Award Nominations for *Girl Wi*

Nominated for the Carneg
Longlisted for the UKLA Boo
Shortlisted for the Hounslow Junio

Praise for *Girl with a White Dog*:

'Jessie is a strong lead character and how she learns about Nazi Germany is turned into an interesting and moving tale' Martin Chilton, *The Telegraph* The Best Young Adult Books of 2014

'A clear and compassionate plea for tolerance.' Nicolette Jones, *The Sunday Times*

'[A] beautiful, moving book about refusing to take the easy path.' Imogen Russell Williams, the *Metro*

'A thoughtful and emotionally charged story.' Julia Eccleshare, *Love Reading*

'Our heroines (and the reader) are faced with many decisions about their own attitudes to prejudice and their ability to stand up for what they feel is right . . . a novel with a powerful punch.' Clare Morpurgo, *School Library Association*

'Powerful and thought-provoking.' Alexandra Strick, Booktrust Book of the Week

'Compelling, well paced and sensitive, this is an (almost) entirely believable novel of our times.' Jane Sandell, *The Scotsman*

'A sensitively-told tale, beautifully written.' Marie-Louise Jensen, *The History Girls*

'It raises issues, challenges prejudice and I know it will stay in my thoughts for a long time. It's a novel that definitely punches above its weight – I loved it and I'd encourage everyone to read it!' Annie Everall, *Carousel*

'Moving and thoughtful, *Girl with a White Dog* should be in every school library.' Zoe Toft, *Playing by the Book*

'Beautiful, touching and important. I loved it.' Nikki Sheenan, author.

'*Girl with a White Dog* is a compelling and candid début novel, which manages to be both challenging and comforting.' Melanie McGilloway, *Library Mice*

'This quietly powerful book is simply told, very accessible and will provoke lots of thought and discussion.' Joy Court, *The Reading Zone*.

'This is such a lovely, thoughtful book and although told in a gentle style it has a powerful impact.' Anne Thompson, *The Bookbag*

I adored this book and cannot wait for more people to read and adore it too.' Kirsty Connor, *Overflowing Library*

'A book which will completely devastate you with its brilliant voice, wonderful plot, and massively important messages.' Jim Dean, *YA Yeah Yeah*

'This is a book that's going to be part of every school library for a long time to come . . .' *Little Wooden Horse*

'This book will change the world.' *Rhino Reads*

GIRL WITH A WHITE DOG

ANNE BOOTH

Catnip

To my husband Graeme and my children Joanna, Michael,
Laura and Christina. Thank you for everything x

CATNIP BOOKS
Published by Catnip Publishing Ltd
320 City Road
London
EC1V 2NZ

This edition first published 2014

5 7 9 10 8 6 4

Text copyright © Anne Booth, 2014
The moral right of the author has been asserted.

Cover design by Pip Johnson
Cover illustration by Serena Rocca www.serenarocca.blogspot.it

A CIP catalogue record for this book is available from the British Library.

ISBN 978-1-84647-1810

Printed in Poland.

www.catnippublishing.co.uk

A STORY TO CHANGE
HEARTS AND MINDS

Write a Modern Fairy Tale

Once upon a time there were two cousins, both princesses.

Princess Fran was really pretty with golden hair and blue eyes, and she lived in a big house in the country with a huge garden and a swimming pool and a really sweet black-and-white cocker spaniel called Charlie. She went to a posh boarding school.

Princess Jessie lived in a much smaller house in a village and went to the local school. She didn't have a dog, even though she had asked for one every Christmas and birthday for as long as she could remember. Princess Jessie's hair was more brown than gold, though Princess Fran once shone a torch on it and said she could definitely see some golden glints. Which was kind, even if it wasn't true.

The princesses' grandmother lived in a house near Princess Jessie. She loved the two cousins very much and had lots of pictures of them on her walls (which they found very embarrassing). And they loved her very much too, because she was kind and loving and made delicious apple cake.

7

And then things went wrong.

Strangers came to the village and did jobs Princess Jessie's father could do, but for less money. And they sat at her bus stop, talking in a different language, and went about in gangs.

Princess Jessie didn't like them at all.

Her father's business went bust. He had to go abroad to work, and the bank took their house back and Princess Jessie and her mother had to go and rent a really small dark house in the village.

And it was all the strangers' fault.

Things weren't too good for Princess Fran either. Her father didn't lose his job – but everyone said he lost his mind, because he left Princess Fran and her mother and went off with someone else. That was when Princess Fran came to Jessie's school.

And so Princess Jessie made three wishes.

1) To have her father home again

2) To stop living in the horrible dark house

3) To have a dog (because she had always wanted one – and still did)

Having all those wishes come true would be her happy ending.

I don't know what wishes Princess Fran made. She doesn't really talk to me that much any more.

My name is Jessie Jones. Mr Hunter, our English teacher, told us to write our own fairy tale. That was my first go. I've always loved fairy tales and I couldn't wait to start writing one.

I knew that a lot of fairy tales don't start very well. There's often something sad, like someone dying, or being lost, or losing their home, before it all comes right and the wishes come true. That made sense to me. It was the perfect homework.

You see, at the beginning of this story, I really did have three wishes. It was easy to imagine that having them all come true at once would be my happy ending. I just didn't realise how sad the beginning would have to be.

Chapter One

We went to Gran's as usual after school on Thursday. I rang the doorbell, and I was sure I could hear barking, which was weird as Gran didn't have a dog. She opened the door with a big smile, but I could see she was disappointed there were only two of us.

'Hello Jessie, hello Kate!' she said. 'Is Francesca not coming again?'

'No, I think she's got a rehearsal or something,' I lied, because I couldn't face telling Gran that her other granddaughter preferred to catch the bus into town after school and hang around with her really annoying friends rather than visit our grandmother. (Who was just as lovely as she had always been. It wasn't Gran who had changed.)

'Oh dear, what a shame,' said Gran, looking sad, but then she hid it behind another big smile.

'Anyway, it's lovely to see you both. Come along inside. I've got a surprise to show you.'

Gran turned and brought Kate and me through the

sitting room, past the millions of framed photographs of me and Fran and the rest of our family on the walls and on the mantelpiece, into her spotless kitchen. There, in a little dog pen, looking out at us with huge dark eyes, was the most beautiful puppy you have ever seen. Seriously cute. He looked like a tiny, snow-white wolf, but with ears that were too big for him and an extremely waggy tail. He was whining and scrabbling at the door, his tail wagging, desperate to get out and see us. Gran opened the door and he ran straight to Kate's wheelchair. He put his paws on her foot rest and she bent down and picked him up.

'Gran – he's adorable!' I said. 'Where did you get him?'

'His name is Snowy,' said Gran, ignoring my question.

I couldn't believe it. It was the best thing *ever*. After a really rubbish year, one of my biggest wishes in life was coming true. I had asked for a dog on my Christmas list from the time that I could write. Every birthday I asked for a puppy – and every birthday Mum and Dad smiled and said, 'maybe when you're older' or, more recently, with more frowns and sighs than smiles, 'dogs cost a lot to keep, Jessie'. When Dad lost his job I thought that my chance of ever getting one was finally over. And now Snowy was here – practically mine. It was like Gran was my grandmother and my fairy godmother all at the same time. Definitely a wish come true.

'We must take good care of him, you and Kate and

Francesca and me,' she said. 'I'll need lots of help. There is so much to do in the garden. I don't know where to start.'

Kate and I looked out at the garden. It was beautiful. Neil from Gran's church came twice a week to do it. There was a smooth green lawn, flower beds and a summer house at the end. I loved the white roses climbing over the walls, and the little fountain. What was Gran talking about? It was perfect – like something in a magazine.

'It looks lovely, Gran. Are you worried the puppy will spoil it?'

She looked back at me and her face changed. She looked . . . I think the best word is *frightened*.

She said, 'No, we have no place to hide them, Jessie. What are we going to do?'

'Who, Gran?'

'I didn't want Snowy shot. I don't want any of them shot. This time will be different. We'll make sure of that, won't we, Jess?'

I didn't know what to say. Who had wanted to shoot Snowy? What was Gran talking about?

'Gran,' I started, and I could hear my voice coming out all panicky, but Kate suddenly passed me the squirming, wriggling puppy and shook her head at me.

'I love your cakes, Mrs Jones,' said Kate, really quickly. 'You must give me the recipe for that chocolate one you make.' Kate can be very charming when she wants to be and she *is* great at cooking, so Gran started talking baking and, as if by magic, changed back into the calm, efficient Gran I knew. Relieved, I looked down at Snowy. I couldn't believe that I was holding a real, live puppy in my arms at last.

The rest of the evening went well. We ate Gran's delicious shepherd's pie for dinner, followed by her yummy apple crumble and custard. And it's amazing how busy you are with a puppy around, putting him in and out the garden so he doesn't have an accident on the carpet (and mopping up when he does). Gran was her usual self and I could have believed all the stuff about shooting dogs was in my imagination, if it hadn't been for Kate being there. Once Kate hears something, she never forgets it.

Then Gran said we could take Snowy with us to Kate's house to show her mum. So we loaded up Kate's wheelchair and we sat in the back. Kate held Snowy in a blanket on her lap, all curled up in a sleepy little heap. We were so busy admiring Snowy and stroking his soft fur and smelling his sweet puppy smell that we weren't paying attention to where we were going – we never usually needed to as Gran had driven Kate the short trip home loads of times.

I suddenly looked up and noticed we were on the motorway. We should have been going down the pretty country lanes near Kate's house, not passing lorries.

I leaned forward to get Gran's attention.

'Gran, why are we on the motorway?' I asked.

I could see her give a start as she realised where she was.

'Jess. I don't know. What do I do now?' she asked.

I think those were the scariest words I'd ever heard. I thought for a minute she'd forgotten how to drive, but she hadn't. She knew how to drive, she just didn't know where she was going. Kate, as usual, knew exactly what to do.

'Mrs Jones, you can take the next exit. It's just coming up now.'

Gran indicated and we left the motorway, heading for Oaksham, a market town about a twenty-minute bus ride away from the village. It was a relief to get away from those lorries, but it was still very frightening. Gran was driving very slowly and her face looked as if she was having to concentrate really hard to listen to Kate's directions. Eventually we saw Oaksham Sports' Centre.

'Ah, good, this is where I go to do sitting volleyball,' Kate said, really chattily, as if it was the most normal thing that we were going there now, at eight o'clock on a Monday night. 'Just turn in here, Mrs Jones – it's the sports centre car park and I've texted my mum that we're going to be here.'

Gran drove in and parked and, as she switched off the ignition, we all breathed a big sigh of relief. Then she put her head in her hands.

I rushed out of the car and round to the driver's seat and put my arms around her. Gran was shaking.

'I don't think I can drive you home, Jess. I'm so sorry,' she said. 'Everything has just gone blank in my mind. It's like a fog.'

'It's OK,' Kate said from the back. 'Mum is coming for me and she's bringing Jessie's mum. She'll drive you both home.'

I sat with my arms around Gran. Her face was so tired and, somehow, young. Suddenly I had a glimpse of her as a terrified little girl. She looked into my eyes like she was trying to find an answer and shook her head as if she couldn't quite believe what was happening. I held Gran's hand and I stroked her hair. I couldn't think what else to do.

Chapter Two

'So Mum and I ended up staying overnight with Gran and looking after the puppy and Mum's taking Gran to the doctor's this morning. I'm really worried about her, Fran. It was so weird. You should have seen her.'

I had tracked my cousin down to the girls' loos before school.

'Gran's probably just tired,' Fran said, checking herself in the mirror. Not that she needed to – she always looked great. 'I'm sure she'll be fine. And the puppy will cheer her up. You worry too much, Jessie.'

I didn't know how to reply because, basically, this is true. I *do* worry too much about everything. Everyone is always telling me that. But that doesn't mean there aren't things you should worry about. And I think if your gran forgets how to drive and gets lost taking your friend home then that's one of them. And she was Fran's gran too.

But by the time I had thought of that, Fran had gone to meet up with her friends.

'You must look after her,' Mum had said to me when we found out that Aunty Tess had taken Fran out of her boarding school and was sending her to mine at the start of the year. Aunty Tess had said Fran needed to be closer to home after her dad left, but Mum wasn't sure.

'It'll be hard for her to settle in after all she's been through,' she'd said. 'I can't believe Mark wouldn't keep paying the fees. I think this may be about what Tess needs, not poor Fran. It's such a shame.'

So Kate and I said we'd look out for her, but, honestly, we needn't have bothered. By the end of the first week, Fran had fitted right in. She was brilliant at every subject without seeming to make any effort and, unlike me and Kate, she managed not to overdo it by showing any uncool enthusiasm.

I'd been at the school right from Year 7, with Kate and most of my Year 6 primary school class. I was still best friends with Kate, and there were a few other people we hung out with, but Fran quickly made me feel like I had joined the school after her. Right from the start she was really confident and smiley and good at things.

For the first few days Fran got lunch with me and Kate and sat with us in the form room, but then, after she mentioned that her dad worked as an accountant for a record company, she became part of Lucy and Nicola's group, and from then on she queued with them, she sat at the back with them, she went into town with them, and it was like we didn't exist. We'd been used to Lucy and Nicola and their friends ignoring us – I just didn't expect my own cousin to. I did try and talk to Fran about it once, but she laughed as if she didn't know what I was talking about, so I just felt silly and stopped.

And she never came with us to visit Gran. Which Kate said was fine by her, because she was fed up with Fran – and when Kate gets fed up with someone it's very hard to get her un-fed up. And I said it was fine by me, too. But it really wasn't.

I left the loos and found Kate by the lockers.

'How's your gran?' Kate asked.

'I don't know how Gran is. She was still asleep when I left. Snowy was awful last night, Kate. He whined so much when we tried to put him to bed downstairs that Mum and I had to drag his pen into the sitting room and sleep on the sofa bed downstairs so he wouldn't wake Gran up. Mum says that's exactly what the books say we shouldn't have done, but she was too tired to care.'

'But he's so cute, like a little white wolf toy!' said Kate.

'Yeah, he is, but I still don't understand why Gran got him. She's never mentioned wanting a dog before,' I said, packing my books into my bag.

'Well, anyway, it's good you've got a puppy now. We can look after him to help your gran out. It'll be great.'

Kate is definitely not a worrier. It's not that she doesn't care, she just thinks bad things can be changed. She's always rushing around saving the planet and getting people to sign petitions. I think she will be a journalist when she grows up. Or Prime Minister. Every day my inbox fills up with petitions she sends me to sign:

URGENT APPEAL!
This [*rainforest / stray dog / remote tribe / hospital*] **is about to be destroyed. Please help us SAVE IT by** [*signing this petition / emailing your MP / ticking this box*]

I do try to read them, but, to be honest, sometimes it's just quicker to type my name and email address in whatever box there is and click *Send* and not bother finding out what I'm protesting about. I trust her. Often, a few weeks later, I get an email from some save the turtles (or rainforests, or planet) organisation saying, *Congratulations! We've done it!* It's a bit embarrassing when I'm not exactly sure what I'm being congratulated for.

I know that Kate says you shouldn't just follow the crowd, but people like Kate just know what to think and what the right thing to do is. They're not scared of anything. They read loads and know stuff. I'm not even sure what biscuit I like best, and I'd rather read or write, or even practise clarinet, than watch the news. The way I see it, some people are good at knowing about petitions and stuff like that and others are good at signing them.

We're always being told to play to our strengths.

We had Maths first, so Kate was in the brainy set with Fran (not that they'd sit anywhere near each other), but we were all together for History after break.

'As you know,' said Mrs Brady our History teacher, 'our topic until the end of the summer term is going to be the Second World War, and today we're going to get on with preparing our oral history projects.'

Mrs Brady showed us some clips of old people talking about their childhoods and told us that we had to go and interview our elderly relatives about wartime life in Britain.

Kate put up her hand.

'What if you aren't from this country and don't have family to ask?'

That was typical of Kate. She wasn't asking a question for herself – Kate is as English as you can get. She was asking for Yasmin, who had joined our class as an asylum seeker from Afghanistan. Yasmin's really quiet and spends most of her time in the library – and that's all I know about her, even though we've been in the same class since she came in Year 8. I looked over at Yasmin and she was staring at her desk. I think she felt a bit embarrassed being talked about in front of the class. I would if it was me.

'I suggest that those of you who don't have relatives or neighbours to interview team up with those who do,' replied Mrs Brady.

Kate put up her hand again.

'My mum organises activities in a care home. I'm sure we could ask the manager if a group of us could interview the people there.'

'Brilliant!' said Mrs Brady. 'I'll get the information from you after the lesson, Kate, and we'll see if you can get that arranged. Anyone who would like to interview someone at the care home Kate knows about, can stay behind.'

After the lesson Yasmin and Ben Green stayed behind and the four of us signed up to interview the residents of Rose Lodge, providing that was all right with the home. It turns out Ben Green's grandparents all live abroad. Yasmin told Mrs Brady that her grandparents are in Afghanistan, and Kate told her that her grandparents were all dead.

'I'm sorry to hear that, Kate,' said Mrs Brady, sympathetically.

'Well, they're as good as dead,' said Kate. 'I don't know my dad and Mum's parents didn't want anything to do with me and Mum when I was born, so I don't see why I should talk to them now anyway.'

I could see Mrs Brady didn't know what to say. Kate often has that effect on people, I've noticed.

'Well. Right, that's settled,' she carried on. 'As you don't have grandparents to interview, you four can do your interviews at Rose Lodge.'

I was glad she didn't get around to asking me about that as, unlike the others, I had a perfectly good British grandparent still alive, but I didn't want to admit that in case Mrs Brady said I had to interview her. Mum's mum and dad are dead – they had died before I was born – and Dad's dad, my lovely Grandad, was dead, that was true. But Gran was here in the same village and English through and through, with the sort of voice you hear on Radio 4.

Only I'd never asked her about her childhood, and I didn't want to now. I wasn't sure why. I just grew up knowing that you didn't. Dad and Aunty Tess never talked about it, and I think Mum once said to me that Grandad had asked her never to ask Gran about her past, as she had bad memories, and, somehow, even when Fran and I were little we knew there were some things we shouldn't say. We could ask her about gardening, or how to knit, or bake a cake, or about any of the many photographs of Dad and Aunty Tess when they were little. But me asking her about what she did as a girl would be as impossible as . . . well, as asking Snowy to talk.

Chapter Three

'What are you going to do about interviewing a grandparent, Fran?' I said when I saw her at the water fountain after History. 'Gran never wants to talk about her childhood. Do you want to come to Rose Lodge with us?'

'No,' said Fran. 'It's sweet of you, Jess, but I don't need to. I've got Dad's dad. Grandad Ken was in the Navy in the Second World War, so I've got no problem. I'll get Dad to take me to visit him this weekend. But have fun at Rose Lodge!'

Written down it sounds fine. I mean, she even said it was sweet of me. But it was horrible – smiley and polite, but distant, like she didn't know me, or really want to know me any more – like we hadn't played in paddling pools as toddlers or laughed until we cried together at family parties about Charlie's doggy farts, or shared a bed and listened to Gran reading us fairy stories to go to sleep.

'What did she want?' said Kate behind me.

I felt really cross. Why did Kate always want to know things?

'Actually, Kate she's my cousin, not yours. We have every right to talk.'

Not that we *had* talked really, but Kate didn't know that.

'What about?' said Kate.

'You wouldn't understand,' I snapped.

'What do you mean? What wouldn't I understand?'

'It doesn't matter.'

I hadn't really thought this through very well.

'You can't just say that. You can't just say it doesn't matter when it obviously does. I just wondered if it was about your gran. There's definitely something the matter with her.'

I could see Kate looking really upset, but instead of that making me stop I suddenly really wanted to do something, *anything* – even hurt her – so that she would stop talking to me.

'There's nothing wrong. She's just tired. And she's *our* gran, not yours.'

I could see Kate sit back and sort of stiffen in her chair when I said that. I had *never* said anything like that before. I had never even thought it before. I didn't really think it now. I knew that Kate didn't have a dad or grandparents or cousins. I knew that my mum and dad and my gran really loved her. I'd always been really glad about that. But I just wanted to get rid of the ball of worry I had inside about Gran, and throwing it at Kate was better than having it inside me for a moment longer.

'What I *do* understand that you're being incredibly mean, Jessie Jones, and I want an apology,' she said, wheeling herself off in front of me to English, our next lesson.

'Everything OK there, Kate?' asked Mr Hunter, the coolest teacher in the school, as we came in.

'I just feel a bit sick. Could I go outside for some fresh air please?' said Kate, pointedly looking away from me.

'Of course. Jess, would you like to go with her?'

'No, I'll be fine on my own, thanks, Mr Hunter,' said Kate, loudly.

'Are you sure, Kate?' Mr Hunter looked concerned.

'Perfectly, thank you,' said Kate, sounding sure and confident and calm, which is how she reacts to feeling rubbish. Not like me. I go red, my lip wobbles and I get all tearful. I really try not to. I'd like to be able to hide my feelings, but I just can't. So I went to my place and kept my head down and hoped nobody could see I was trying not to cry.

A few minutes later Kate had to wheel herself over to her place next to me, which she did without making any eye contact. She took out her pencil case and put it on the table and looked straight ahead at Mr Hunter, who was writing on the whiteboard.

Once Upon a Time, he wrote.

'Can anyone tell me what we associate those words with?'

'Fairy tales, sir,' said Nicola Barker, who made it so obvious she fancied him. Mr Hunter *is* gorgeous, but I would have died rather than show it like Nicola did. She had a way of flicking her hair back and pushing her chest out in his lessons, which you never saw when we had Chemistry with old Mr Peters.

'Exactly. When we hear those words a whole set of associations come with them. Can anyone tell me some of the things you expect to find in a fairy tale?'

The whiteboard soon filled up with suggestions. Catherine Parks suggested handsome princes and looked over at Callum Andrews, which was a bit obvious, though he didn't notice, as he was too busy flicking paper balls at Shona Williams. He's been flicking paper at Shona since we were at primary school, but she always ignores him. Shona Williams suggested beautiful princesses. Fran said talking animals. William Lewis and Rory Black, when Mr Hunter dropped a big hint about films like *Lord of the Rings* and *Harry Potter* having fairy tale elements in them, said about castles, wizards and dragons. Carl Davis said the word 'pumpkin' as if it was the funniest word ever. He has a really weird sense of humour. Lucy Banks, speaking in a bit of an irritating baby voice, said about magic spells. Everyone seemed to be suggesting things. Everyone except me and Kate. Me because all I could think of was Gran forgetting how to drive and being so small and frightened. And also because I was so aware of Kate, still staring angrily ahead on my left. And Kate because it seemed to be using up all her energy glaring into the air at nothing so that she had none left over to answer questions.

'Jess. Any suggestions?' Mr Hunter smiled at me. He has the best smile of all our teachers. He is definitely the nearest thing to a handsome prince we have at school.

I felt so chewed up. I knew that my best friend was sitting beside me, feeling really really hurt, but I felt like I couldn't unsay the words that caused the trouble, because then the conversation would unravel back to the beginning, and everything would be horrible again. I needed to stay in a world where everything ends happily, where Gran would have a nap and be back to normal by this evening.

'Happy endings?' I blurted out.

'And why, Jess, do we need fairy tales to have happy endings?' said Mr Hunter.

'Because if it doesn't end happily and if everything isn't all right, then what's the point? It's all horrible and there's nothing you can do about it.'

And then, to my complete embarrassment, I burst into tears.

And I felt Kate's arms around my shoulders.

'Her gran's ill,' I heard her say.

'I'm very sorry to hear that,' Mr Hunter replied. I was too embarrassed to look up. 'Would you like a little time out, Jess?'

I couldn't look at him, instead I looked at the desk and nodded.

'Perhaps Kate would like to go outside with you for a bit? You could maybe sit in the courtyard garden for five minutes. We're going to be watching excerpts from some Disney fairy tale films, and then talking about happy endings, so come back in when you're ready.'

I passed Fran and the rest of the cool gang sitting at the back as we went out, but she didn't look at me. Our school has a small courtyard garden, with a bench and some rose bushes and a little fountain. It's just off the corridor next to our form room and it's a designated 'quiet area'. It was made when a sixth former got killed in a car accident a few years ago. Normally it's out of bounds for anyone below the sixth form, unless a teacher says they can use it. People go there when they have problems. This time it was me with the problem, as I sat on the bench and bawled my eyes out. And then I said sorry to Kate.

'Well, I'm sorry I made you talk about it,' said Kate. 'Mum told me not to.'

'No, I'm sorry, Kate. Gran really loves you. She always says you're her third granddaughter. I don't know. I just hate Fran being so different. And I'm scared.' I blew my nose on a tissue Kate gave me. 'Everyone seems to think that Gran's just tired. What if that isn't it?'

But Kate didn't have a chance to tell me what she thought.

'Thanks a lot, Jess!' It was Fran, who had appeared out of nowhere in the courtyard. She wasn't smiling at me patronisingly now. She wasn't smiling at all. 'You've really embarrassed me.'

'What?' I asked.

'Overreacting like that about Gran. It's so typical. Why do you have to be such a drama queen about everything? Mr Hunter knows we're cousins, so he asked me if I was feeling worried about Gran too. I had to pretend I wanted to cry so that he wouldn't think I was heartless. Why do you always want to be the centre of attention?'

'That is so untrue!' said Kate indignantly. She's a real best friend.

'What do you know?' said Fran. 'I'm fed up with it. I care about Gran too, but it's stupid getting so worked up when she just needs a rest. You're a cry baby, Jess. Just grow up.'

'Everything all right, girls?' said Mr Hunter, coming out into the courtyard.

'Fine,' said Fran. 'I think we feel a bit better now, don't we, Jess?'

How patronising could you get?

There wasn't much I could say and we followed Mr Hunter back into class.

'So,' said Mr Hunter, '*Grimms' Fairy Tales* were German folk tales collected by two brothers – Jacob and Wilhelm Grimm – and published in 1812. These old stories had already been handed down over centuries through the oral tradition before the Grimm brothers wrote them down. I'm going to hand out one for you to read now, and I want you to think about the elements we have talked about, plus any possible message you can find.'

The story Mr Hunter gave us to read was *Little Red Riding Cap*, the old name for Little Red Riding Hood. The wolf reminded me of Snowy, although obviously *a*) Snowy can't talk and *b*) he isn't evil – even if he does chew everything. Little Snowy would have just licked Red Riding Cap and Grandmother, which would have been a lot better.

Then I noticed there were two wolves in the Grimms' story, which was strange. The first wolf is killed by the woodcutter, but the second comes afterwards. This time Red Riding Cap recognises he is trouble straight away and she and her grandmother trick him with the smell of sausages so that he falls down their chimney into a trough of water and drowns.

A happy ending . . .

'What's the message of this fairy tale then?' asked Mr Hunter.

'Don't talk to strangers?' said Nicola Barker.

'Be careful the same thing doesn't happen twice?' said Ben Green.

I thought that was really good. Ben has a way of noticing things and putting them into just the right words. I see him at orchestra every week. He only joined our school last year, and I've been a bit shy about talking to him, but I like listening to the comments he makes and how he makes everyone laugh. He's really good at funny voices. And he's really good at trumpet.

'There were two wolves,' Ben continued. 'But at least the second time Red Riding Cap recognised the danger and didn't have to rely on being rescued.'

'Good, Ben. OK. I think it's time to give you your homework. Only, I'm a little worried you might not be brave enough for this particular story,' Mr Hunter joked. 'Not too scared?'

We laughed, and I saw Carl Davis smirking over at Fran and her friends, and doing a big elaborate yawn.

'You've got a week to do this homework as it has two parts. The first is to read the Grimms' fairy tale, *The*

31

Robber Bride, which I'm about to give you a photocopy of. Think about the discussion we've had and write a paragraph on whether this fairy tale has a happy ending. The second part is to write your own fairy tale. It doesn't have to be sweet like Disney – you can write a gruesome one like the Grimms. Now don't read *The Robber Bride* too late, I warn you . . .'

He smiled at me as he said that, and I got a bit flustered. Basically, I went bright red, and then I tried to flick back my hair like Nicola Barker – I'm not sure why – I think I had some vague idea it would make me look more sophisticated or something. Then I rocked back in my chair as he gave me the handout, fell flat on the floor and everyone laughed. Of course, Mr Hunter then helped me up, which was really embarrassing and really exciting at the same time as I got to smell this really lovely aftershave he wears. I went even redder and wanted to die. I was so relieved when the bell rang.

Chapter Four

'Careful, Jessie, don't fall off your chair!' said Fran as I was sitting down in afternoon registration, making everyone laugh again just when I was starting to forget about it. My cousin had become scary funny. You didn't want to do anything silly near her, because this new Fran was really good at laughing at you and making everyone else laugh too. She looked pretty when she was doing it, and she sort of said it in a way that sounded really friendly. But it wasn't. It was nothing like the Fran who used to tell me I had golden hair and that we were twins.

I kept getting flashbacks all afternoon. Every time I heard anyone laugh or saw them smile I felt like everyone else was remembering too. Yet another embarrassing thing that Jessie Jones has done. I'd never be cool like Fran.

I was glad when it was time to go home.

When school ended Mum texted me to remind me to go back to Gran's after school. I had the key so I opened

Gran's door and a small white furry ball of legs and wagging tail and licking tongue hurled itself at me.

'Don't let him out, Jessie!' called Mum, sounding hassled. 'Pick him up and come through to the lounge and say hello to Aunty Tess.'

I dumped my bags in the hallway (Gran always insists on bags being hung up, shoes put away, slippers on, but it was an emergency), and picked up Snowy, who was wriggling like mad. It was nice to feel so appreciated, even if it was a bit embarrassing trying to talk to Aunty Tess while my face was being licked. Mum took him from me and went through to the kitchen and put him in his pen.

'He's been an absolute nightmare,' she said. 'We've been trying to arrange things and he's all over the place. I think we might have to give him back to the Rescue.'

'No!' said Gran, coming down the stairs. 'No one is giving that dog back to the Rescue.'

'But, Mum,' said Aunty Tess. 'I can't take him with poor old Charlie being so ill now, and we've agreed that you need to come to us and rest for a while. He's such a lovely puppy, someone else will adopt him – he's a bit too much of a handful for you.'

'No! No!' Gran was seriously upset. 'Jessie can look after him while I'm away, can't you, Jessie?'

'But Jessie's at school, Elizabeth,' said Mum. 'And Dave's in France and I'm at work. It wouldn't be fair.

34

And the landlord would never let us have a dog.'

Gran came over to me and took my hands in hers. They were trembling.

'Please, Jessie. Please don't let them take him. I'll be back soon. Please, promise me.'

I looked into her eyes and I saw the same fear that I had seen in the car. I would have done anything to take it away.

'It's all right, Gran, I promise. I'll look after Snowy until you come back.'

'Good girl,' said Gran, and stroked my cheek. She looked so pleased that I knew I had said the right thing, although I had no idea how I was going to do it.

'I think Jess and I had better move in here then for the time being,' said Mum. She was biting her lip in the way she does when she feels really fed up, but is trying not to show it. She's done that quite a lot since Dad's business went wrong. 'There's no way we can bring him back to ours.'

'Right, well, that's settled then,' said Aunty Tess. 'You look after the dog.'

She sounded quite relieved and I could tell Mum was making a real effort not to lose her temper with her. Mum says we should be patient with Aunty Tess because of Uncle Mark, so she's been really trying to be nice about her, but I know she used to say Aunty Tess could be a bit selfish. She looked like she was thinking that again now.

'I think we'd better go now, Mum,' said Aunty Tess to Gran. 'Fran will be delighted to see you. She's catching a later bus because she had choir rehearsal, but she's very excited about you coming.'

I doubted that. Excited. Fran didn't do excited any more. And what choir rehearsal? Kate and I were in choir and there wasn't any rehearsal tonight.

Aunty Tess picked up Gran's suitcase and Mum helped Gran out to the car.

'I'm sure you just need a holiday, Elizabeth,' said Mum. Poor Mum. She looked so tired herself. 'We've got an appointment for you for Monday. A bit of spoiling this weekend and Tess's cooking won't do you any harm. We'll look after the garden while you're gone.'

'Jessie will do the garden, not you,' said Gran.

Mum looked a bit hurt. 'I know I'm not a very good gardener but . . .'

'Jessie, you know what to do,' said Gran. 'You must clean out the shed. Plant bushes. There weren't enough last time.'

I could see Mum and Aunty Tess exchanging looks over Gran's head. It was really weird. Gran wasn't making sense, but her eyes were really focused and she seemed to know exactly what she was saying and expected me to understand. I felt like I was in some role play exercise in drama class.

'OK, Gran.'

'Good girl.' She smiled and stroked my hair and gave me a kiss.

'I'll bring her back for her appointment on Monday,' said Tess. 'I still say it's disgusting that she couldn't be seen in the doctors' today. I read in the papers it's all the people coming from abroad – I don't see why they should get in ahead of a British person.'

'To be fair, I don't think anyone, British or not, got a last-minute appointment. They're short-staffed at the surgery since Dr Petkov left,' said Mum, but you could see she didn't want to continue talking about it. Aunty Tess can get very worked up about things she reads in the newspapers. 'Anyway, we'll see you on Monday, Elizabeth. Bye Tess, thanks. I'll ring Dave.'

Then Aunty Tess helped Gran into the car and they drove off.

'Honestly,' said Mum. 'I do love Tess, but she does go on . . . Anyway, what was all that about you gardening with Gran?'

I could tell Mum was trying not to mind about Gran telling her not to help.

'Gran has been telling me about jobs she needed to do in the garden, that's all,' I said. That lie cheered Mum up and she led the way into the kitchen, where she made me a cheese sandwich and I poured us out some juice, both of us trying to ignore the frenzied scrabbling and whining coming from the pen.

'I could take Snowy for a walk up the hill,' I said, sounding like I was just trying to be helpful, but actually wanting a chance to spend extra time with him. 'I know where Gran keeps the lead.'

'That sounds good,' said Mum. 'He probably needs exercise. It might tire him out and it would let me go and move our things over. Thanks, Jess.'

Chapter Five

It was a bit tricky fixing the lead on to Snowy's collar, especially as he kept jumping about, but I managed it and led him down the path. Actually, it was more like him leading me. He pulled and panted and wagged his tail and when I stopped to open the gate to the field behind Gran's house he nearly strangled himself trying to get through. He stopped to do a wee and then set off again. I almost wished I had roller skates on, or some sort of adapted water skis – field skis for puppy walking. If you could harness puppy energy, you could solve the energy crisis.

I was just imagining telling Kate about millions of puppies fixing global warming when disaster struck. One minute I was being pulled up the hill by a puppy, the next I was holding an empty lead. I mustn't have attached it properly after all.

'Snowy!' I yelled. I looked up and down the hill. How could a puppy just vanish like that? It was such a relief when I saw him, but he was bouncing about with something dead and horrible in his mouth. He ran to me wagging his tail, but he wouldn't drop it, keeping just far enough away that I couldn't grab him easily. I knew I had to get it off him before he started to eat it.

'Snowy! Come here boy!' I called.

'Turn away from him when you're calling him, and run down the hill,' came a voice. It was Ben Green. He seemed to have appeared out of nowhere.

'Make yourself more interesting than what he's got!' And Ben started running and making funny faces and waving his arms and yelling, 'Snowy!' in lots of different silly accents.

He paused and looked at me.

'Come on, Jessie!' he yelled, and somehow I found myself waving my arms and jumping up and down like a mad thing too. The next thing I knew Snowy was beside us, without the horrible thing in his mouth, then Ben was holding him in his arms and making a big fuss of him.

'He's gorgeous. Is he yours?' said Ben, as I carefully attached Snowy's lead again.

'No, he's my gran's. I'm looking after him for her,' I said.

Ben seemed very close as we both tried to get Snowy to stay still – I hadn't realised his eyes were so green and smiley, or how his hair flopped forward. I could feel myself getting redder and I was glad that we had just been jumping about so it might not have been obvious I was blushing.

'Is that OK now? I've never attached a lead before and I don't want him to run off again,' I said.

Ben checked it. You could tell he knew what he was doing. 'You should come to dog-training. My mum's a vet, but she runs a class in Bluebell woods every Saturday. It's really good fun.'

'Great!' I said. To be honest, if Ben had invited me to a bungee-jumping class I would have agreed.

'Well, it's tomorrow, one o'clock – I'll be there. We meet at the car park entrance? You'll be able to see all the puppies.'

Ben opened a little wooden gate beside the path that I hadn't noticed (which explains where he came from).

'I live here, so bye then, Jess. Maybe see you tomorrow?'

He disappeared into a garden and I could see his house right at the end. So, I was going to be going past Ben's garden up that hill every day with Snowy. And seeing him on Saturday for dog training.

When I got home Snowy settled down in his basket and fell asleep. He looked so like a little white wolf. I wanted to reach out and ruffle my fingers through his coat, but that might have woken him up and I needed a rest too. Mum was back, but I could hear her on the phone to Aunty Tess, so I knew she would be ages. I found some biscuits in Gran's cupboard to keep me going until dinner, made myself some hot chocolate, then settled down in Gran's armchair and started trying out ideas for fairy tales. I doodled some pictures of castles and an enchanted wood, and a magic dog and a princess, and I tried out a story about me and Fran, but I didn't get very far.

'Everything all right?' said Mum, who was looking tired after getting off the phone. 'Poor Tess,' she said, without waiting for me to answer. 'Uncle Mark turned up unannounced, saying he'd come to take Fran to his parents for her school project. And he had his girlfriend in the car with him. Apparently he'd arranged it with Fran and she hadn't told her mum anything about it.'

'Did Fran go?'

'Yes. I suppose he is her father, after all. But Tess is very upset.'

'How's Gran?'

'Tess says she's sleeping. I'm glad she's got her check-up at the doctors' on Monday. We'll just get the weekend over with.'

I sighed. 'Does Dad know about Gran yet?'

'Yes, I rang him. You know Dad. He always looks on the bright side. He says Gran's probably just been overdoing it.' She looked at me. 'Come here, Jess, let's have a hug. Thanks for taking Snowy out tonight. That was a big help. I think we should splash out and get a takeaway for a change, what do you think?'

So Mum went out and got a Chinese takeaway while I practised clarinet, then she came back and we snuggled up on the sofa and watched *Enchanted*, which was about fairy tales, with great songs, lots of laughs and a happy ending. I felt like a little kid again.

'Thank you, Gran,' I said out loud as I settled down to sleep. Snowy looked up and wagged his tail. He was sleeping in my room after whining so much when we turned the lights off downstairs. 'And thank you, Snowy.'

I couldn't quite believe my luck. Three fantastic things had happened. Ben Green had talked to me today. (I don't think he'd ever actually said my name before.) We would be going to Rose Lodge together in a group. And tomorrow we would be spending the whole afternoon together!

Chapter Six

And then it was six o'clock in the morning. I heard piteous whimpers and scrabbling at the wire door.

'He'll wake up early to wee. Are you *sure* you want him in your room?' Mum had said, and I had absolutely promised I would get up. So now I had to leave my lovely warm bed and stumble my way across the room to get him.

'Snowy, you're a pest,' I said, but it was hard to be cross when he was so soft and warm and pleased to see me, licking my face and wagging his tail when I opened the door to pick him up. He was very wriggly as I carried him downstairs, my face in his soft, white, teddy bear fur, but I managed to hold on to him until we got out to the garden. He scampered off and I hopped up and down in the cold until I saw him do a satisfyingly long wee on the grass. Then he bounded up to me and I made a big fuss of him and brought him inside. He kept me warm as he curled up next to me on the sofa and we watched some of the cartoons I used to watch when I was little. Mum came down and we made our breakfast as Snowy ate his and then charged around with a squeaky plastic bone in his mouth.

'Whatever happens,' said Mum, 'we've got to puppy-proof the house. I don't think Gran really knew just how much damage a puppy can do. I don't know what got into her.'

We heard the post drop onto the mat and I raced Snowy, his tail wagging wildly, to the hall and scooped up the envelopes before he could jump on them.

'Thanks, love,' Mum said, sifting though the pile. She picked up a postcard. 'Oh look, this is a lovely picture!' She turned it over. 'They must have sent it to the wrong address.'

She handed me back a postcard. On the front was a painting of an outdoor market in the snow, with ladies in headscarves and men in hats and children wrapped up warm against the cold. It wasn't a modern picture, but it wasn't like a grand old one in a gallery either. I could see a girl and a white dog trotting along beside her. It was addressed to Gran's house, but to someone called 'Maria Bayer'.

I read the handwriting. It was in biro and easy to read.

Grandfather told me to tell you the gallery is still there, waiting.

'It's a shame, but I don't think there's any point in putting it back in the post,' Mum said. 'They haven't put a sending address and the stamp is German. I wonder how they got the address – Gran has lived here for over fifty years.'

I really liked the painting. In a funny way, it reminded me of Gran. She always loved markets and snow. It looked like a happy, busy place. I turned it back over again to see if it there was any information on the back. The printed description was in German, but I could only work out that it was about a marketplace and that it was painted in 1930. (Which was probably best not mentioned to Fraulein Bonhoeffer, our German teacher.)

I didn't really know what to do after I helped Mum clear up breakfast, but I didn't want to start on my homework, which I knew would be Mum's suggestion if I said anything.

'Shall I go and find the person the card is to?' I said. 'I could go up the post office and ask them if they know.'

'If you like. Take the card with you and I'll get on with things here,' said Mum. 'I'll ring Dad and then I'll move some of Gran's more precious things out of the way. Thank goodness Snowy has fallen asleep. And if you really don't mind taking him to that puppy class you mentioned, I can nip out after lunch and get some shopping.'

She sighed and for a moment I wondered whether she might want some help, but sometimes it's best to just let

Mum get on with things herself.

I love our post office. It's a shed tacked on to the side of the Rose and Crown pub right at the end of the village near my primary school. Carl Davis' mum was a bit of a local heroine, because when the old 'proper' post office closed years ago and got made into a house, she got the pub to let her open this little Wendy house one. It's very small, but she's put bunting around it and window baskets outside to make it like a little hut of treasures. It was always a treat when we were little to go there after school and buy sweets or pots of bubbles or something from her bargain bucket. There's always a queue at the counter because Mrs Davis likes chatting so much. She knows all the village gossip, so I bet she'd know who Maria Bayer was.

I stopped to read a few postcards in the window before I went in. Two people were advertising for work as builders and I knew both of them – Lucy Banks' dad and Shona Williams' big brother. Callum Andrews' sister Laura was offering babysitting, and someone else was selling a car. There were hens and ducks, which I really wished we had a garden for, and a card for *Greenfingered Gardening*, which was Gran's friend Carol and her son Neil. Carol drove him to people's gardens and he did the work.

I could hear Mrs Davis shouting before I got through the door. Not cross shouting, but the way she talks to

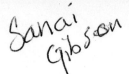

people who aren't English. One of the foreign workers was at the counter.

'I CAN'T TRANSFER MONEY FROM HERE,' Mrs Davis shouted. 'IT ISN' T SECURE. YOU NEED TO GO TO A BANK IN TOWN.'

'For my family. I am sending it to my family,' he said.

'YES. BUT YOU CAN'T SEND IT HERE. GO TO A BANK. IN TOWN. SAFER.'

'What? For my family? I send here?'

'YOU NEED TO GET THE BUS. TO TOWN. BANK,' shouted Mrs Davis. 'TOO MUCH MONEY IN CASH. BETTER BANK TRANSFER. OK? I CAN'T HELP YOU.' Then she looked past him over his shoulder at Rory Black's mum, who was next in the queue. The man walked past us out of the hut, shaking his head.

'Did you see how bulky that envelope was? There must have been an awful lot of cash stuffed in that. You can't help wondering where he got it all,' said Mrs Davis.

'He's one of the farm workers, isn't he?' said Mrs Black. 'I imagine he's been saving.'

'I don't think they're paid enough to save much – and from what I hear most of their money gets spent on cheap beer. How's your oldest son? At university, isn't he?' This was typical Mrs Davis – she never stayed on one topic for long.

'Yes. He's studying in Poland this term. I wanted some stamps for this letter to him.'

'Is he really? Nice to hear one of us going over there for a change instead of the other way round. He must be doing well. Lovely boy! Your Rory must miss his brother. I know I couldn't let my Carl go abroad when he's older. He won't even go on sleepovers, he hates leaving home so much. He's a real mummy's boy,' beamed Mrs Davis.

I couldn't wait to tell Kate about mummy's boy Carl. I bet he would have *hated* hearing his mum say that. I wished I could record it and play it back to him when he was being annoying.

I looked in the bargain bucket whilst Mrs Davis sorted out things for Mrs Black. I used to love the colouring books she sold when I was little, but now I had my eye on a special shampoo to 'bring out your natural blonde'. I know I'm not really blonde but I thought it was worth a go.

'How can I help you, Jessie dear?' said Mrs Davis, as Mrs Black left. 'How's your poor Dad doing in France?'

'He's fine, thanks, Mrs Davis. But we got a postcard sent to Gran's and we don't recognise the name. It's to a Maria Bayer. Do you know anyone?'

'Maria. Let me see.' This was the sort of thing Mrs Davis loved. She is always one of the main people in the village pantomime, so she knows how to be dramatic. She held the card up to the light, put her glasses on and off, twisted it round and over.

'I suppose it could be Mrs Baker. Try Mrs Baker.' She nodded with approval at her own suggestion. 'I think she might be a Mary. The lady in the big old house next to the old post office.' She passed it back.

'Could I take a look?' said Mr Jones, who had appeared behind me in the queue. Every November he stands outside the post office in his old soldier's uniform and sells poppies. Gran always buys a poppy for each of us – including Fran – from him.

'It could be a Mrs Maria B. Ayer, of course. I believe there is a Mrs Ayres in the white cottage next to the shop. There might be a simple spelling mistake. You could knock there,' he said, as he handed it back to me.

I thanked them both and bought the shampoo. Then I went and knocked on old Mrs Baker's door, but she said the postcard wasn't for her and she didn't know anyone who might be on holiday in Germany.

When I got to Mrs Ayres' house Neil was there gardening out the front, but he said she was out shopping. Neil has Down's Syndrome and he's been gardening in our village as long as I can remember. Gran always gives him a big hug whenever she sees him. Neil gets very worried and upset about people he loves getting ill – his mum said to my mum that he couldn't sleep when Gran went to hospital to get her hips done a few years back, so I thought I shouldn't say about Gran not being well.

I decided to settle for putting a note through Mrs

Ayres' letterbox. Mum's always complaining how I never empty my pockets, but I find it comes in really handy. This time I found an old toffee and a pen, so I unwrapped the toffee and popped it in my mouth (it tasted fine), Neil found a piece of paper in his bag and I scribbled a note, asking Mrs Ayres if she was expecting a card from Germany and letting her know where to find it if she was.

When I got back, Mum answered the door looking very stressed. Snowy was bouncing around on his lead. He was really pleased to see me, and so was Mum.

'I am so glad you're back, Jess. He's been awful. I let him out because he kept howling in his pen. Then I thought he was in the garden, but he'd got upstairs and under Gran's bed when I wasn't looking. He's pulled this box out and chewed it – I caught him before he completely destroyed it, but look!'

On the dining room table was a cardboard box, wet and torn.

'It looks like it has private letters in it, and old photographs,' said Mum, sounding upset. 'I feel so bad because it was obviously important to your Gran.'

I took the lid off. Inside – basically OK, but still a bit wet – were lots of blue airmail letters and postcards and small black-and-white photographs. The first one I picked up was a photograph of a very thin and serious looking girl of about fourteen with a beautiful white German Shepherd dog that looked like a grown-up version of

Snowy. There was something about the girl's face that made me want to look at her more.

'Mum! Do you know who this is?'

'I don't know,' said Mum, taking it from me and looking at it. 'Dad always told me he had never seen any photographs of your Gran's family.'

We turned it over but there was no name.

I started to look through the other photos, but Mum stopped me.

'I think we should wait until Dad comes back and look at it together. I'll find another box and put the things in it and keep it safe somewhere.'

Mum went to get a new box, and I looked again at the photograph of the girl and the dog. I had this weird, overpowering feeling that the girl in the photo was looking at back at me, telling me she didn't want to go back in the box. Her eyes met mine as she sadly hugged her dog.

I put the photo in my pocket.

Chapter Seven

After lunch Mum drove me to Bluebell Wood with Snowy. There was birdsong *everywhere*. I know it might sound stupid, but I was amazed at how green it was. The trees towered above and even the air felt green. The light was streaming down like we were in some cathedral full of stained glass – I thought that I wouldn't mind doing a painting of it.

I could see a group of people waiting a bit down the path from the car park.

'Are you sure you'll be OK?' said Mum, as I struggled to get out before Snowy, who, in scrabbling to escape my arms and the car, was strangling himself on the lead. I knew Mum was relieved to have Snowy out of the house and desperate to go and buy some stairgates before Snowy wrecked everything. Poor Mum. She works all week in the bookshop and I was sure she could have thought of a better way to spend a Saturday afternoon.

'I'll be fine. See you at three,' I said, and she drove

off. Actually, I felt a bit sick. I wasn't exactly an expert on puppies and my arms already felt pulled out of their sockets by Snowy. I strongly suspected he'd be better pulling a sledge than on a lead. Added to that, Ben Green was here. My heart was beating faster the closer I got to him. I felt like I was going into an exam I hadn't prepared for. I walked closer and closer to the group of people with puppies and realised I had no idea what to say.

Luckily (though I didn't think it at the time), Snowy broke the ice by pulling so hard as we got near the other puppies that I let go of him. 'I'm so *so* sorry!' I said, over and over again, as I ran up to try to disentangle Snowy – barking, wagging and bouncing all at the same time – from the other excited puppies, (now all barking too, thanks to my dog) and their leads. It was like a chaotic cat's cradle or a May pole dance gone terribly wrong, with dogs yelping and owners calling their names – the sort of thing you see on YouTube and laugh at unless it's happening to you.

I was bright red by the time Ben dived in and retrieved Snowy.

'I'm so sorry,' I said to Ben's mum over Snowy's excited barking. Even if I hadn't heard Ben calling her 'Mum' I would have guessed who she was as she had his green eyes and dark hair. She was small, and wore a green jacket and wellies and jeans. It was a bit scary how she somehow managed to restore order so that each owner and puppy were standing at a distance from each other.

'Don't worry!' she said, taking Snowy's lead from Ben and magically getting him to be quiet and sit next to her with some manoeuvres involving the lead and a treat. He seemed very surprised to find himself at her feet and looked up at her as if she was this amazing goddess. She didn't look at him and kept talking to me, but slipped him another treat while he was sitting, which he was very pleased about. Dog treats. I didn't have any. I was doomed.

'It's Jess, isn't it? Ben mentioned you'd be coming. And this is your gran's puppy? Shall I work with him today?' Her voice was really American, which surprised me, as Ben sounds so English. She was quite stern, almost like a soldier, and I would have been a bit frightened of her if she hadn't eventually smiled at me. She had a very nice smile, one of those ones that transforms someone's face.

'Oh, yes please!' I said, and watched as she turned a wildly over-excited blur of white fur into this amazingly alert, attentive little dog. It was like he was hypnotised by the treats she had in her hand. She didn't make a fuss of him, or pat him. She just walked him ahead of the others, giving him quick, firm jerks on the lead whenever he tried to pull ahead, and a little biscuit whenever he was walking to heel, so that Snowy walked up the woodland path with the others like a model puppy.

'She's like a magician,' I said to Ben, watching her with awe. One good thing about our entrance being so cringe-making was that I didn't have time to worry about talking to Ben. I had used up all the embarrassment I had. Ben smiled at me and I felt much better. Maybe this could be fun.

'She's been doing it all her life,' said Ben. 'Her mum was a vet in America and she grew up with lots of dogs.'

'Do you have a dog?'

'Yeah, we have a few.'

You could tell just by the way he said it that he really liked animals.

Ben's mum kept Snowy with her but shouted instructions to the owners struggling to walk their puppies up the path.

'Good to see Spike's enthusiasm, Julie – typical terrier!' she said to an older woman being pulled up the path by a panting little dog with a rough, scruffy little coat. 'Keep twitching that lead and getting him to walk to heel.'

There was a smiley man called Karim, with a big black labradoodle puppy called Trudie. Ben told me that the shaggy-looking, waggy, bouncy, mongrel puppy with two small children and their mum was called Jumble.

'Well done, Janice,' Ben's mum said to a woman with a beautiful golden cocker spaniel. 'Champagne is walking very well today,'

'That's a posh name!' I said to Ben.

'Thank you,' said Janice, who thought I was talking to her. 'It's actually Champagne Pretty-girl Flower-puppy, but we just call her Champagne.'

Luckily she had walked off before Ben and I glanced at each other and nearly burst out laughing. I suddenly felt this was going to be a *great* day.

We got to a clearing at the top of the path, just where the path forked in two, and Ben's mum stopped.

'Right, playtime,' she said. 'Fingers in collars and release.'

Suddenly all the puppies were running around and jumping on each other, including Snowy.

'Will they be OK?' I said to Ben.

'Yes – look at their tails. No aggression there.'

He sounded very knowledgeable. I was glad he was there otherwise I would have worried. To be honest, I was just glad he was there full stop.

'Now, let's keep walking,' said Ben's mum. 'Don't call them yet – they should be looking to see where we're going and keep up with us.'

And they did. If I was going to make Ben's mum into a fairy tale character I would definitely make her into the Pied Piper, but with dogs. She led a line of dog owners, who were followed by loads of puppies, wagging their tails and rolling over and sniffing and cocking their legs, but all close on our heels. It was really cool.

Ben looked over at me as we were walking and cleared

his throat. 'Um. Kate asked me something a bit strange. She asked if rescue centres put down dogs they couldn't rehome, and she said your gran said she had to rescue Snowy because they were going to shoot him,' he said.

'What?' said Ben's mum, coming up behind us. 'Who were?'

'I don't know,' I said, feeling a bit self-conscious as everyone was looking at me. Thanks Kate, I thought. Why did you have to blurt that out to Ben of all people? And now his mum was announcing it in her very loud, outdoorsy sort of voice.

'That sounds very odd to me,' said Ben's mum. 'He looks like a perfectly healthy, normal puppy. And dogs aren't shot when they are put down these days. There must have been a misunderstanding.'

I nodded, hoping everyone would stop talking about it. Snowy ran up to us wagging his tail, as if he knew we were talking about him.

'Isn't he a White Shepherd?' said Karim, bending down to give him a pat. 'I wanted to get one, but my wife fell in love with labradoodles.'

'White *German* Shepherd,' said Ben's mum. 'My mother used to breed them. She'll be joining us next week, so don't let her hear you call him anything else! She's very particular.'

Meanwhile, Snowy had bounded off again for more fun.

We got to the end of the path and watched the puppies run about the clearing. I panicked a bit at first when Snowy jumped on top of the other puppies, but Ben's mum was almost scarily relaxed about it and Ben told me that was just the way puppies were and they would soon sort it out amongst themselves – which they did. At one point I saw Snowy at the bottom of a squirming pile of puppies, but he emerged wagging his tail, his tongue hanging out, and promptly started another puppy rugby scrum.

Janice, Champagne's owner, was frantically trying to pick the leaves or mess off her puppy every time she came near. She obviously couldn't quite believe that the puppies weren't going to kill each other.

'She's a pedigree show dog,' she said to Ben's mum. 'I didn't know the lesson would be like this. I think this is too rough for her.'

Champagne herself looked completely up for it. She was wrestling with Snowy at the time, and winning.

'You must let the puppies play. I will intervene if necessary,' boomed Ben's mum.

'She cost thousands. Her relatives showed at Crufts!' protested Janice.

'At Crufts, don't you know!' mimicked Ben under his breath.

I laughed and had to pretend I was coughing.

'Mongrels are rougher than her,' said Janice, as she

tried to separate Champagne from Trudie the labradoodle and Jumble the mongrel.

'Stop that!' said Ben's mum very suddenly and loudly. 'Let the dogs play together!'

'Pardon?' said Janice, looking shocked and upset. It was a bit embarrassing, because you could see she was blushing and near to tears about being told off so publicly.

'Oh dear,' said Ben watching his mum glare Janice into obeying her. 'Mum's got a thing about mongrels being as good as any other dogs.'

Karim went over to Janice, and they walked together for a while. Champagne charged off and was obviously fine, so I think Janice calmed down. I noticed she kept well away from Ben's mum though. I wasn't surprised – I felt like avoiding her and I wasn't even the one who was getting told off.

Although that was a bit awkward, the rest of the morning was brilliant. Ben helped me do some training with Snowy. I managed to drop Snowy's lead and get him to stay for about five seconds, which was pretty rubbish compared to what the others could do, but they were really encouraging. And, to be honest, having Ben next to me, stroking Snowy and making me laugh, was the best bit of all. I felt like I could talk to him normally at last. He even did a cheeky impersonation of his mum when I was getting into a tangle with Snowy.

'Keep it up, Jessie. You'll make a dog trainer yet,' he

said in an American accent. His mum turned round, but she just laughed and wagged her finger at him. I think my mum would describe her as having a bark worse than her bite. (Though I'm not sure if Janice would have agreed.)

Everyone thanked and paid Ben's mum, loaded up their dogs and drove off, leaving just me and Snowy waiting for Mum to arrive. Ben's mum told me not to worry about paying for the session.

'I think you're doing a good thing looking after him while your gran is ill, so I'm glad to help out. He'll be a great dog as long as you're consistent and firm.'

Then the mobile rang. It was Mum. Her voice sounded really shaky and breathless.

'Jess. I'm so sorry. Can I speak to Ben's mother for a minute? There's a bit of a problem with picking you up. I wondered if she could keep you and Snowy for a while?'

'Mum, are you OK? What's happened?'

I could see from their faces Ben and his mum had heard what I said.

'I'm fine, Jess. It's your gran. She's had a bit of an accident and I'm in the hospital with Aunty Tess and her. Could I just speak to Ben's mum? Don't worry darling – everything will be OK.'

But it wasn't. Not yet.

Chapter Eight

Mrs Green drove me to the hospital where Mum was standing outside the entrance anxiously looking out for us. She told Mum not to worry *at all* about Snowy – that he could easily come home with them. Then she drove off with Ben holding Snowy on his lap. The green woods an hour ago already seemed like another world. Now it was all echoey floors and lifts and Mum and me walking fast down long white corridors to my gran.

Mum told me on the way that Gran had got up in the night at Aunty Tess's to go to the loo, forgotten where she was and taken the wrong way to her room, falling down the stairs. Aunty Tess had been in Accident and Emergency with her most of the night, and in the ward all morning, and had only just gone home for a rest.

We got to the door of Gran's ward, squirted the disinfectant stuff on our hands and were buzzed in by a nurse. As soon as we pushed the door open I heard Gran even before I could see her. She was at the entrance to her bit of the ward, out of bed and shouting.

'You can't keep me here! I insist on going home – I'm not staying here to be murdered.'

She was standing up in a white hospital gown. There was a long tube coming out of her hand attached to a bag of fluid on a stand and the nurses were trying to get her to stay still so that she didn't pull everything over. She was pushing at them and swaying on her feet.

'Mrs Jones, please calm down. You'll pull the drip out. You need to come back to bed and rest. You've had a nasty fall and we've got to check you out before we can let you go home,' said one man, while the other nurse stood behind Gran, I suppose to catch her if she fell.

It was horrible. I'd never seen Gran like it before. She was like a little old lady drunk.

Gran saw me coming in the ward and called out.

'Jessie! You'll help me. They want to keep me here to murder me. They're going to inject me. You've got to help me.'

We both went up to Gran, though I had no idea what to do. Then she reached out her hand to me and as I took it, she gripped me very tightly. She looked so small and scared.

'It's all right, Gran,' I said. 'We're here now.' She let us persuade her back into bed, but she wouldn't let go of my hand. It was beginning to hurt, she was gripping it so hard.

'I wish I'd helped, Jessie,' Gran whispered, and I saw that she was crying. 'I didn't know. I thought it was all lovely. I didn't know what was happening. And now it's happening to me. Help me.'

The nurse tucked her in, but Gran ignored her. She just kept looking into my eyes as if I was the only person in the world.

'Gran, the nurses aren't trying to hurt you. They're trying to make you better.'

Gran shook her head.

'No. That's what they told us, but it wasn't true. I should have known. I didn't want to hear. I should have known with the dogs. The dogs and the cats and the canaries. Jessie, I need some paper and a pen. Please. Quickly.'

Mum rummaged in her handbag and passed me a notebook and a pen. Gran took it from me and, her hand trembling really badly, wrote the letters *JM* on each of three pages. Then she ripped the pages out and gave them to me.

'Give one of these to Kate, and one of them to Fran, and tell them to keep it with them always. Especially Kate. If they come, tell Kate to sit on the sofa. Not the chair. Say you'll get the buttons later. Choose your friends carefully.'

I looked at the pages. The letters didn't even make a word. Why on earth would we need to have them?

What buttons? It would have been funny if Gran wasn't so upset.

'OK, Gran,' I said, folding them and putting them in my pocket. I couldn't think of anything else to say.

She pulled me closer and whispered, 'Where is Snowy? Is he safe?'

'Yes, Gran, he's fine.'

'Did you get him to the woods?'

'Yes. He had a lovely time.'

'And the others were there?'

'Yes. Lots and lots of them. They were really happy, playing together.'

'Lots of them? And they are all safe?'

'Yes, they're really safe.' I tried to sound confident and reassuring even though there was a tight knot of worry in my stomach.

'They're safe.' She sat back against the pillows and repeated it as if it was the greatest relief in the world. 'And happy?'

'Yes, they had a great time.' Why was she so interested in puppy training?

'You're a good girl, Jessie.'

I looked over at Mum.

'Everything is going to be all right, Elizabeth,' Mum said, but suddenly Gran was asleep – it happened so fast that I panicked for a second until I saw her breathe.

'She's tired herself out,' said Mum. 'Apparently

she's been shouting like that most of the morning. The doctors say it's because of the fall, and that it often happens like that.'

The family visiting the middle-aged lady next to Gran gave us tight-lipped smiles in return for our apologetic ones. Obviously no one in their family had ever shouted in a ward.

Gran didn't wake up for hours after that. The nurses came and went and adjusted her drip and took her temperature. Machines beeped, and a doctor came and talked to Mum about shock and rising blood pressure and X-ray results, low potassium levels and fluid levels and infections. I wandered down to the vending machines and the hospital shop for sandwiches, crisps and magazines for Mum and me.

'Do you want to have a break, Mum?' I said, because she looked so pale and tired and worried.

'Are you sure, Jess?' Mum said. 'I would love some fresh air. I'll only be a quarter of an hour away, tops. Call a nurse if you get worried.'

So Mum went and I sat by the hospital bed, looking at Gran tied up to drips and looking so papery and frail. I closed my eyes.

'Please, please make Gran better,' I prayed in my head. Suddenly I felt Gran's hand on mine and I opened my eyes. She was looking at me and for one blinding moment I thought that it had happened. A miracle.

Then Gran spoke.

'Jessie. I am so glad you're here.'

'I'm so glad I'm here, too, Gran.'

'How is Snowy? He's such a clever puppy.'

'Yes, he's lovely,' I said. I felt relief run through me. Everything was going to be fine. I wished Mum was there to see it.

'Yes,' said Gran. 'You could even teach him to talk.'

What? This wasn't good.

'I had a cousin who worked in a college for dogs who were learning to talk,' Gran went on.

'Pardon, Gran?' I said. Her voice was quite faint but she was determined to go on.

'A college. My cousin Heidi worked there with very clever dogs. They were going to teach them to talk, and do guard duty.'

'And did they?' I said. I couldn't think what else to say.

'No, but I think they nearly did.'

'I've . . . I've never heard of your cousin Heidi,' I said, trying to get off the mad subject of talking dogs before anyone else heard.

'I don't see her any more,' said Gran. 'I don't want to see her again.' Then she closed her eyes.

Maybe I should have asked her more then. Maybe I should have told Mum and Aunty Tess and the doctors and nurses what she had said before we left, but I wanted so much for my prayer to have been answered. Gran had been shouting and fighting, then I had prayed and now she seemed so much calmer. She was tired so she was saying a few odd things, but basically she was lovely, normal, kind Gran again. My wish had come true.

Or that was what I told myself . . .

Chapter Nine

I woke up the next morning, smelling coffee and bread and hearing a very familiar voice . . .

'Dad!'

I rushed past Snowy's empty pen (I must have slept right through him waking up) and downstairs to see Dad sitting at the breakfast table, leaning back against the wall, long legs stretched out. Mum was sitting cuddled up to him and smiling. He got up and gave me a big hug – in fact, Mum joined him and she and Dad both gave me a Jess huddle-cuddle – a sandwich hug like the ones they gave me when I was little. Normally, I'd have reminded them that I wasn't a kid any more, but I just felt like enjoying it. And with an excited furry blur of white puppy trying to get in on the action, there was happy chaos for a few minutes.

There's often happy chaos with Dad. He's always thinking of great things to do. And I could already see Mum's anxiety melting away having him beside her. If some people are 'glass half empty' people, Dad is 'glass half full and I'm sure there's another bottle somewhere, it's just a case of looking for it' sort of person.

'I've finished the house, I've driven all night to see my girls, and I'm hearing good news about your gran already,' said Dad, now with an enthusiastic Snowy on his lap, who was wagging his tail and wriggling and trying to lick his face. 'Aunty Tess texted me to say Gran had a very good night and they are talking about her going home tomorrow.'

'Home? Here? Already?' Mum looked a bit panic-stricken.

'Yes. It's going to be fine. Don't worry. I'm going to take time off work. We can all stay here for a couple of weeks with her to make sure she takes things easy and isn't worn out by this little fella,' he said, putting Snowy firmly down on the floor so he could give Mum a reassuring hug.

Snowy rolled on his back immediately, twisting his head and looking up at my parents with floppy ears, big dark puppy eyes and tongue hanging out as if to charm them by sweetness. They laughed. Snowy was working his magic again.

After breakfast we took Snowy up the hill. It wasn't the woods, but it still felt magical. It was so quiet as we walked up the side of the field towards the top. Nobody else was about, as if the whole human world was still asleep, like in *Sleeping Beauty*. There was wheat or something growing in the field, wild flowers on its edge by the grassy footpath. I should really know what they all were because we did a thing about them in Brownies years ago, but all I could say was that there were little yellow ones, some daisies, spindly blue ones, and some gorgeously red poppies. It was one of those blue sky early-summer days, with clouds like you draw them in pictures – ridiculously cotton-wool like – and birds singing. It was perfect.

'Name that birdsong, Jess,' said Dad.

'Er, blackbird?' I guessed wildly and (by luck) correctly, according to Dad. In my bedroom I've got a clock Gran gave me one Christmas, which plays a different birdsong every hour, and it's a family joke that I'm learning each one by heart in my quest to be a TV wildlife presenter one day. The trouble is, by the time an hour has gone by, I can't remember what the earlier bird sounded like.

Dad's different. He's so good at all that stuff. He loves camping and walking and looking at nature. And, surprisingly, for someone so neat and organised at home, so does Gran. When we went camping together, it was always Mum who got in a despairing mess with the tent, while Gran and Grandad ran it like a military operation. Gran set up the tent area with little washing lines to air the sleeping bags during the day, comfy fold-up chairs for us and always plenty of clean mugs and a kettle.

Grandad would make a fire while she would cook amazing dinners and generally create order out of muddle just like she did at home. She didn't even seem to get muddy if it rained. If you went into their tent, everything was folded neatly and easily found. In ours you could just hear Mum swearing and hitting her head against things.

It's been a few years since we went camping together. Not since Grandad died, and that was when I was about ten. I suddenly really missed them, Gran and Grandad together. Why did things have to change?

I looked over at Mum, walking along, hand-in-hand with Dad. She looked so much younger now he was home. Dad's magic was working just like Snowy's.

'Do you think Gran will be well enough to come on dog walks soon?'

'Sure she will!' said Dad, cheerfully. 'She just needs a bit of a rest.'

We passed Ben's back gate and my heart started beating a little faster. A tiny bit of me wanted Snowy to wriggle under the fence so that we would have to call on them again, but the rest of me was relieved when Snowy kept charging on in front of us towards the top of the hill. His back legs were almost too fast for his front, so he kept looking as if he was going to fall over.

We sat down on the bench at the top of the hill and looked down on Middlebourne. It was like a story-book illustration. You could see Gran's house, and the other big houses with their gardens; the High Street with the butcher's and the baker's, the greengrocer's and the chemist's and Mr Gupta's corner shop; the Rose and Crown pub and the post office hut. Middlebourne Primary School lay beside the village playing fields and we could see little figures running around the football pitch. I knew it was too far away to see, but I couldn't help squinting in case I could make out Ben down there. The river shone as it ran through the meadows and there were sheep in the fields next to the farm, with a few caravans for the farm workers who came over every year. Off to the right was the main road, with the distant sound of lorries and cars somehow making the quietness of the hill more special. Then, as if it wasn't magical enough already, the sound of the church bells from St. Mary's started up.

'Isn't England beautiful?' said Dad, sitting on the bench with Mum on one side and me and Snowy (now on his lead) on the other. None of us said anything about the fact that down in that lovely village scene, one of the big houses used to be ours. None of us said anything about the awful day when my parents told me Dad's business had gone bust and the bank was taking our house to pay off the money he owed. Nobody mentioned how Mum cried, and how Dad apologised. And how Aunty Tess came over and blamed all the foreign workers for undercutting Dad's business.

'Leave it, Tess, you're not helping,' Dad had said tiredly. That was a day when even he knew his glass wasn't half full.

Afterwards, when we'd moved from our lovely big house to the tiny rented cottage on the other side of the village, where none of our old furniture would fit, and Dad was away working in France, I saw the foreign fruit pickers outside the corner shop, I couldn't help remembering what Aunty Tess had said. I told Mum I didn't like the way the foreign workers spoke their language together in the street, or at the bus stop, or sat on the benches in the playground.

'Where are they supposed to sit, Jess?' said Mum, but I knew she didn't like me cutting through the playground on my own when they were there. We didn't know them. They didn't speak our language, and hung around in groups. And that was scary.

When we got back home after our walk, Dad asked me to go to Mr Gupta's to get the newspaper, some gravy granules and a packet of bread sauce.

'I'm going to do a roast today before I go to the hospital. And get your mum a magazine – one of those glossy ones she likes.' He gave me some cash. 'Get yourself something too.'

Having Dad home made things so much better – I wished the reason wasn't that Gran was ill, but I was glad he was back. I just wished Gran could be better and Dad could stay so things would be like they used to be.

My phone rang. It was Kate.

'You know when you and me and Yasmin and Ben were all chatting after History and I said about going to see a film together one day?'

I did know, because I remember thinking I would never have been able to suggest that to Ben in a million years. Although, actually, maybe I could after this weekend.

'Mum says she can give us a lift to the cinema this afternoon if we want. She asked Yasmin's family and they said yes, and I phoned Ben and he says yes too. Do you want to come? Mum will drop us home.'

Kate was amazing – she knew how much I liked Ben. Of course I wanted to come. This day was getting better and better.

Mum and Dad said that I could go to the cinema after lunch instead of visiting Gran and I texted Kate my reply on the way to the shops. I felt a bit guilty, but also secretly relieved. If I didn't see the hospital I could pretend Gran wasn't there.

Mr Gupta was serving some of the fruit pickers when I got there. I walked past them to the newspapers and magazines. The headlines on the Sunday papers in Mr Gupta's were pretty gloomy. It was funny how they were practically all the same. I counted two headlines about there being no money for jobs, one about 'bogus asylum seekers' taking our money, and one about there being

76 - Friday

no money to pay for looking after old people. The one which Dad wanted just said there was an economic crisis. It was much more fun choosing Mum's magazine. Lots of the magazines said you could lose weight with a special diet, or share the make-up secrets of the stars, although it seemed to be a different diet and a different star for each magazine, so all I can say is there must be a lot of secrets (and some of the stars definitely looked better than the others). I knew Mum liked the ones with country kitchens and pretty bunting and hampers on the covers so I chose one with no diets, but a free lipstick worth twenty pounds, which had to be a bargain.

I got myself some chocolate from the display at the checkout and left Mr Gupta's feeling really cheered up. Everything was going to be fine. Dad was home and Aunty Tess had said Gran was getting better. It was OK if I went to the cinema and didn't visit today. She'd be home soon. But just as I passed the bus stop near Mr Gupta's I saw Neil, Gran's gardener, crying, bent over trying to clear up four flowerpots smashed on the ground, earth everywhere.

'They pushed me hard when I got off the bus, and I dropped my plants and then they laughed and called me a very bad name,' he said. It was awful. I could see he was shaking.

I knew already who'd done it. It was the fruit pickers – they were always at the bus stop.

77 – Friday

It wasn't fair. The day had been so nice up to now – and now they'd spoiled even that. Those foreign farm workers were always hanging about, but how mean could they be, pushing about someone like Neil? I suppose they thought it was funny.

Everything had been fine before they came. First they took my dad's work and now they were hurting people I loved. I just wanted them to go back where they came from.

Chapter Ten

'Please. I clear up.' I turned to see one of the foreign workers standing with a broom and a bin bag behind us. 'I get from corner shop.'

'Why did you do it?' I said. 'Why did you pick on him just now?' I glared at him.

'Sorry?' said the man, frowning as he tried to understand me.

'No, Jess. Not him. He didn't do it,' said Neil.

They both looked at me.

'Sorry,' I said to the man. 'Thank you, then.' I didn't say it particularly nicely. If it wasn't him, it was his friends, after all. I was so angry.

'Is OK. You OK, then?' he asked Neil.

'Yes, thank you.'

'I help carry. Wait,' said the man. He tied the bin bag and put it in the bin, then ran back to Mr Gupta's shop with the broom.

'Who did it, Neil?' I asked while the man was gone.

'The girls and the boys.'

'Where did they go, Neil?' I felt all fired up and ready to do something.

Neil looked over at Mr Gupta's shop. The man who was helping us was coming out followed by a group of teenagers who were laughing. Danny Williams and Liam Smith from the year above, Nicola Barker and . . . Fran. They must have been in the shop at the same time as me. Typical Fran not even saying 'hello'.

'It was those people,' he said, ducking his head slightly. 'The teenagers.'

'What? Are you sure, Neil? Those girls and boys?'

'Yes. They pushed me over and laughed at me and called me names.'

Oh no. It had been easy to get cross at a grown-up stranger, who had ended up helping us, but when I looked at Danny and Liam with Nicola and Fran I didn't feel so brave.

'Come on, Neil, let's go back to my house,' I said. 'Don't pay any attention to them, they're just stupid.' The foreign man looked at us with concern.

'OK?' he said.

'OK,' I said. 'Thanks.'

'Thanks for helping,' said Neil.

And we went.

And I felt rubbish.

But what could I say?

You shouldn't push Neil. You shouldn't find people funny just because they're different from you?

Like they would listen anyway. Danny and Liam and Nicola would probably have just laughed at me too. Fran? I don't know. I just didn't understand her any more. She might have changed but I never thought she'd bully someone like Neil. What could I have said to my cousin? It was horrible. I felt such a coward.

I walked Neil home to our house. Mum and Dad were really shocked when I told them what happened. They would have been even more shocked if they knew one of the teenagers had been Fran. But they had enough to worry about with Gran, and we'd had such a lovely morning. Besides I really wanted to go to the cinema with Ben and Kate and Yasmin, not get involved with another family crisis. So I didn't say anything. I wasn't lying. It was like the words to tell that particular part of the story just weren't there. I'd talk to Fran later.

Mum and Dad each gave Neil a big hug and said they'd give him a lift home on the way to visit Gran as I got ready for the cinema. I just had time to wash my hair with the new shampoo from the post office. I thought it might make the day seem good again.

❧

'Your hair looks really nice – I can see golden glints,' said Kate's mum when she came to pick me up. She didn't even have a torch to shine on it, so that proved it worked. I like Kate's mum a lot. Ben and Yasmin and Kate were waiting in the car and it was brilliant to see them. We were like a real gang. I started feeling better.

The film was hilarious, but what was even more fun was hanging out with Ben, Yasmin and Kate. Yasmin was different from at school – she looked so glad to be with us. But then we dropped her off at her house and it gave me a bit of a shock. I knew she lived in a bed-and-breakfast, but I thought that meant a lovely little cottage or something. I'd even felt a bit jealous, to be honest. I remember thinking that living in a bed-and-breakfast would be nicer than in our new house. But it wasn't pretty with roses around the door. It was a big old building with peeling paint on the sign and dirty windows.

Ben and Kate stayed in the car and I thought I'd walk with Yasmin to her door. Kate's mum and I waited with her as Yasmin rang the doorbell. It was the man who owned it who answered. He wasn't very friendly – not like the lady in the B&B in the Lake District we stayed in once on holiday – but he let us go with Yasmin up the stairs to her room. I didn't like the dark staircase, and the landing and the corridors smelt bad – a sort of a mixture of cooking food and toilet smells. I could see why Kate's mum wanted to see her safely back. Yasmin's big brother, who is in the sixth form at school, answered the door.

'Thank you very much for taking her,' he said, and Yasmin disappeared into a room which seemed to be full of people. I could hear a baby crying.

'Does everyone in her family live in that room?' I asked Kate's mum as we walked back to the car. It made me feel really strange.

'Yes. It's very tough, isn't it? Yasmin's dad was an interpreter for the British army in Afghanistan. He had to get his family out quickly when they got death threats from the Taliban. His brother was killed so he knew they were serious. He's waiting to hear if they can stay in Britain.'

I felt a bit sad again after that – quite a lot, actually. Kate's mum dropped me home. Even though we had my favourite beans and cheese on toast for tea, and there was good news from the hospital about Gran's blood pressure being lower, that sadness didn't really go. No matter how much I cuddled Snowy or tried to remember the funny bits in the film. I just kept thinking about Yasmin. Then I thought about Gran on her own in the hospital, and about Neil at the bus stop. And about Fran. It felt like my lovely, golden-glinting day had been spoiled, like when the shine gets worn off a new coin.

I told Mum and Dad I was tired and went up to bed. I got one of my favourite comfort books out, one Gran gave me when I was little and which I'd brought over to the house – *Heidi*. I love the story. And Gran had told me she had loved it when she was little too, which was practically the only thing I knew about her when she was a child. I'd read it over and over again, and each time I got caught up in the beautiful world of mountains and snow and Clara and Peter and the goats and Heidi and her kind, gruff grandfather. It even had Clara being in a wheelchair, which reminded me of Kate. Though Kate would be furious if someone threw her wheelchair down a mountain like Peter does with Clara's. And she wouldn't be able to miraculously walk afterwards if he did. Life isn't like books.

Heidi. I thought of what Gran had said about her cousin. And then I thought about dogs and remembered the photo we'd found in Gran's box. I felt under the pillow and brought out the photograph. I wondered why the girl looked so sad as she cuddled her beautiful dog.

'I wish you could tell me what happened to you,' I said, and went to sleep.

Chapter Eleven

'Are you OK, Jess?' said Kate the next morning when we met at the lockers.

'I'm fine,' I said, automatically.

'Are you sure? You don't look it,' she said. And I burst into tears and sat down on the bench next to the lockers.

'I just feel a bit horrible,' I said. 'You know Neil, who does the gardens? Some teenagers pushed him over yesterday.' I still didn't say Fran's name. If I didn't say it, maybe it wasn't true. Though I knew it was. I just didn't know what to do about it. 'And Aunty Tess phoned this morning to say Gran had a really bad night. And Snowy destroyed Mum's slipper at breakfast and she was really angry and stressed, and Dad keeps saying that everything is OK, but I can't see how. I'm worried we might not be able to keep Snowy if Gran doesn't come home soon. Maybe she won't even be well enough to look after him once she's home, and our landlord won't let us keep pets. It's not fair.'

I found a tissue in my pocket and blew my nose. Kate gave me a hug.

'That's awful,' said Kate. 'I'm so sorry. It's turning out be a horrible day for both of us. I just heard that they might not give my volleyball club any funding this year. I know it's not as bad but . . .'

I could tell Kate was feeling really miserable, but was trying to be kind to me. And I really wanted to be kind back, because she was my best friend and this was seriously bad news. Kate is brilliant at sport. She's a fantastic swimmer and she's won medals for archery, but sitting volleyball is special for her. She's only been doing it for a year or so and people are actually talking about her going to the next Paralympics.

'Oh Kate, that's awful. Let's go to the volleyball court after lunch and practise.' (Which showed how sorry I was – I'm rubbish at sport and the last thing I wanted to do was go to the volleyball court. Still, it always cheered Kate up and was better than sitting around worrying about Gran.)

'Thanks, Jessie,' said Kate. 'Though I don't know if that will help. I suppose all this means today can only get better . . .'

Monday morning we have whole school assembly. Mrs Rowlands, our head teacher, looked really pleased about something, and she had a microphone, which always means that she has (or thinks she has) something special to say, like the time she made a *huge* fuss about the fact that we were *each* getting a free apple for lunch as part of a healthy eating week. She also uses a microphone when she's really cross, like when she told us all off for being so rubbish at fire drill, and how if we didn't get our acts together we would all die horrible deaths. Today she was beaming, so it probably wasn't anything bad.

'Do you think we're getting free apples again?' I whispered to Kate. 'I might faint with excitement.'

'Yeah,' Kate said. 'Let's hope they're the green ones this time. That'll make up for *everything*.' Suddenly we both got the giggles. The day seemed a bit more bearable somehow.

Mrs Rowlands tapped the microphone to get our attention.

'We're very proud to announce that we have just heard that one of our Year 9s, Kate Oliver, has been chosen to be on the Junior Great Britain Sitting Volleyball Team, which is a great honour for her but also a huge honour for the school.'

'Hey! That's fantastic, Kate!' I whispered. 'Why didn't you tell me?'

'I didn't know! They must have told the school first.' Kate looked so happy and surprised. I was glad there was some good news at last. Surely they couldn't withdraw funding from her club now?

'A sport where you sit down all the time. That sounds *really* difficult,' I heard Fran say to Nicola Barker. Then they both laughed. I could tell Kate had heard too as she went a bit red. I glared at Fran, but she was just looking ahead again as if she hadn't said anything.

'We'd like to invite Kate Oliver up on the stage, as we have a prize we'd like her to accept,' said Mrs Rowlands.

Kate wheeled herself up the ramp on to the stage. It must have seemed odd, her looking so angry.

'Could I say a word, please?' she said in a loud, clear, very cross voice. Mrs Rowlands looked a bit startled.

'Of course,' she said, handing the microphone to Kate.

'I'd just like to say that sitting volleyball isn't just a sport where you "sit down all the time". Well, obviously it is, but it needs upper body strength and hand-eye coordination and stamina and teamwork and it is a highly respected Olympic sport. And I don't want a prize for being in a team because just being in the team is an honour.'

I looked over at Fran, but she and Nicola were just laughing at Kate getting so angry.

'Well, thank you, Kate,' said Mrs Rowlands, taking back the microphone. 'Actually, we weren't going to award you a prize.'

You could hear a bit of a snigger from around the hall. Kate went even redder. I felt so sorry for her.

'It's better than that,' carried on Mrs Rowlands, saving the situation. 'I am pleased to say that this is a prize for the whole school.' She held up an envelope. 'This letter, which will be put up on the P.E. noticeboard for everyone to read, says that due to your achievement, we are going to get a visit and some coaching sessions from the actual Great British Sitting Volleyball team. So all of you will get a chance to try this, as Kate rightly says, very demanding sport.'

Then Mrs Rowlands gave Kate the envelope and started a round of applause for her as she wheeled herself back down the hall to us, looking really hot and bothered. Why did Fran have to spoil things?

As soon as assembly was over we went to Music. Luckily we had a Djembe drumming session, and even though Kate and I couldn't talk to each other, since Mr Benson put us in different groups, I could tell she was still angry because she really banged her drum hard and Mr Benson had to remind us all that rhythm was more important than volume. I just tried to drum out all the sadness I felt, but it didn't really work. Then it was break, and the P.E. teachers and Mrs Rowland and some other people came up to congratulate Kate, but as soon as she could get away she wheeled her chair out really fast down the corridor. I had to sort of do an awkward trot after her to keep up until we reached Fran, who was standing with Lucy and Nicola by the vending machines, talking to Danny Williams and Liam Smith. I hated seeing them all together. It made me think about Neil and the bus stop again.

'Hey, Fran, what's your problem?' called Kate. 'Why the sneery comments about sitting volleyball?'

Fran turned round, looking very relaxed. Not like Kate, whose knuckles were white as her hands gripped the armrests.

'Sorry?'

'Why did you say all that stuff about sitting down?' said Kate. Her voice was getting louder and louder and people were looking over at us.

'Well, you do sit down, don't you? No offence, but who's interested in being coached in sitting volleyball? It's not exactly a mainstream sport.'

Nicola and Danny burst out laughing at something they were reading on a text, and Fran turned her back on Kate to look at it.

'EXCUSE ME!' said Kate. 'We haven't finished our conversation.'

'What?' Fran turned around, as if she had forgotten Kate was there and was really bored to be still talking to her. 'Yeah, well, I think it's really good. It's like Children in Need or whatever.' Nicola and Danny laughed.

'Don't be so patronising,' said Kate. I had never seen her so furious.

'Er, don't get so worked up,' said Fran, 'I just think it's

a shame that we're getting money spent on a visit from a coach for a minority sport when the netball court needs fixing.'

'Well, maybe when you get chosen to be on the national netball team you'll get funding for that,' said Kate. You could see that had really got under Fran's skin – she stopped smiling suddenly and glared at Kate. The only thing Fran had 'failed' at since she'd come to our school was getting past district-level netball.

'Come on,' said Liam Smith, and put his arm around Fran. He said something in Fran's ear which we couldn't hear and they, Lucy, Nicola and Danny all walked off, but then they looked back at us and laughed. I felt myself getting hot with embarrassment. It was horrible.

'Kate – I'm so sorry. I don't know what's got into her. She's just . . . I think she must be jealous. She knows you're a million times better than everyone at sport, even her,' I said.

I was really shocked to see a tear run down her cheek. Kate rubbed it away angrily. The bell rang for end of break.

'Thanks Jess, thanks for trying to be kind.'

'I'm not being kind. Or trying to be – you *are* better than everyone. You're better than me.'

'That's not hard is it?' Kate said, checking her lesson planner.

That hurt a bit, even though I knew it was true.

Living through Kate is definitely the nearest I will ever be to being good at sports. I used to read all those Enid Blyton school stories when I was younger, and I seriously imagined myself scoring the winning goal in a lacrosse match – not that I actually knew what lacrosse was. I just imagined being carried shoulder-high from the pitch or the field or whatever, everyone cheering me. I thought it would all come right for me at secondary school. Instead, in my school reports I get top marks for effort, but bottom marks for actually being able to do anything.

Mum says that 'effort' is the important thing, but that's easy for her to say – she was good at sport. She wasn't ever in a P.E. class where she had to listen to Shona Williams and Lizzie Young arguing about not wanting me in their teams and then, because both of them are actually really nice, explaining, 'We all like you, Jess, but we really want to win.' I stood, last in the hall, wanting the floor to open and swallow me up, but I saw their point. Even I wouldn't pick me.

'No offence, Jess,' continued Kate (why do people always say that when they are going to say something nasty?), 'but I really don't feel cheered up being told I'm better than you at sport. I'm better than most people at sport. It's just that ignorant people like your cousin can't see it. Just because I'm in a wheelchair. I hate it.'

'But you're so good at it,' I said, stupidly. I didn't

actually know what to say. I'd never seen Kate like this, so defeated and upset. She'd always got really cross when people seemed to pity her.

'What does that mean? Good at being in a wheelchair? Don't think I like it, Jess. Don't think I like having to have stupid fights with the bus company just so that I can get to school on the same bus as everyone else. Don't think I'd rather not have to plan ahead for everything just to make sure there's enough stupid disabled access where I'm going. Don't think I like being patronised by your cousin, or when some stupid person complains to Mum about disabled parking. It's just getting worse and worse. You're so lucky. You just don't get it . . . you're just so lucky. You don't have to fight for ANYTHING!'

For a few seconds I just stared at Kate. She had never been that angry with me. My heart started thumping really fast and I couldn't think of anything to say.

Eventually I stuttered, 'But . . . but you won that fight with the bus company. You were in the local paper and everything. It was brilliant. You were brilliant. I thought you liked campaigning.'

'Not campaigning *all* the time! I want to be lazy, to be nice like you, instead of good old campaigning Kate. And, right now, I just want to be alone, Jess. You're really not helping.' And Kate wheeled herself off as fast as she could down the corridor away from me.

93 — Wenesday

I didn't want to burst into tears yet again, but it was hard not to. Great, I thought. We'd had a fight on Friday, and now it was Monday and we'd started again. We never fought. And I'd just been called lazy and nice, neither of which seemed like a compliment.

Chapter Twelve

I was glad that Kate and I didn't have to talk to each other in History. We just sat in silence as Mrs Brady showed us a DVD of newsreel from the Second World War. Very posh English voices told us how the children of Britain were 'stepping up to the mark' and there were shots of evacuees with labels and little suitcases on railway platforms and leaning out of train windows; jerky, smiling figures of girls practising first aid on each other, and children waving into the camera while wearing gas masks. Then she showed us a really odd film of Hitler talking to a big crowd. I couldn't understand why anyone would want to follow him. He was waving his arms and shouting and he had that little moustache and then there were all these soldiers marching in lines with their arms up. It looked ridiculous, and Carl Davis got told off for laughing, but I didn't blame him, even though I was too scared of Mrs Brady to do it myself. Who could take that seriously?

I suppose it was because we'd had over an hour when we didn't dare to laugh in front of Mrs Brady that it went a bit wrong in German, which was next. Fraulein Bonhoeffer is our German teacher. I like her because she never shouts, and I think she's quite young – I've never seen anyone with so many pairs of shoes. She once let Ben and his friends run a competition for Comic Relief guessing how many pairs she has. Including wellies she has thirty pairs. I have no idea how many pairs Mrs Brady has, and I'm sure she wouldn't tell us. Not that we'd be interested anyway.

'Guten tag meine klasse,' Fraulein Bonhoeffer greeted us, wearing a pair of bright red shoes I'd not seen before. 'Please read page ninety in your textbooks whilst I go and get the tests from last lesson.'

In German lessons, after we get the boring stuff done, we normally read and write and talk about modern German families or look at the displays Fraulein Bonhoeffer puts up of castles and forests and cruises down the Rhine. We've even tried some black German bread and some German cakes Fraulein Bonhoeffer brought in. German lessons are fun and I'd already decided to do it for GCSE in Year 10 because Fraulein Bonhoeffer said I had a 'natural aptitude for it' (which I think she'd take back if I told her I couldn't even translate the back of that postcard). But German-lesson Germany and History Germany didn't really link up in my mind. I knew

History Germany was horrible and our enemy during the War, but German-lesson Germany was somewhere I really wanted to go on holiday, a sort of fairyland place with castles and lovely people like Fraulein Bonhoeffer and wonderful Christmas markets.

My only excuse about what happened next is that page ninety was a really really boring page about verbs and we had just watched loads of German Nazi soldiers goose stepping for hours and hadn't been allowed to laugh, which made it funnier somehow, and I was feeling miserable about Gran and Kate and Fran. So when Carl Davis stood at the front of the class with his finger under his nose to pretend he had a moustache and put another arm in the air to do a Nazi salute, then started goose stepping around, I thought it was hilarious. I don't know why, but we all got a bit hysterical, and Ben Green and I started shouting at each other in mock German accents about meeting up to go to Rose Lodge. We were all making quite a lot of noise and lots of us were doing funny goose walks and shouting 'Heil Hitler' at each other. And that's when Fraulein Bonhoeffer walked back in and saw everything.

And it all went silent.

The worse thing was that she didn't even get cross, like Mrs Brady would have done. She just gave back our test papers and we had a really strange hour of calmly going through the answers we should have given and talking about how many rooms we had in our house and how we spell our favourite hobbies. We didn't even laugh when Carl Davis said he collected stamps. I could tell he was disappointed. He wasn't used to us laughing when he mucked about and he didn't want it to end. I don't think we'd ever been that well behaved in any of Fraulein Bonhoeffer's lessons. I felt terrible.

The bell for lunch went.

I saw Fraulein Bonhoeffer again when I was playing clarinet at lunch time orchestra. She plays the trumpet with Ben. They are both really good – I've learned from them that good trumpeters don't puff out their cheeks. I wanted to tell her how sorry I was about what happened in her lesson, but I couldn't think of how to say it. It isn't as if I normally chat to her. She's young and nice, but she's still a teacher. Although, as we were putting away the music stands she came over and talked to Ben and me anyway.

'It's funny, I think of the Nazis every time I play jazz,' she said.

Not Nazis again! I didn't really know what to say. I could tell Ben felt the same. It was really awkward. Fraulein Bonhoeffer could see we didn't know what to do, but she carried on anyway, helping stack the stands as she talked.

'The Nazis banned jazz and swing music. My teacher told me this when I started learning the trumpet when

I was your age. I think he loved playing jazz to spite the Nazis' memory, and now I do the same.'

'I don't think people think about Nazism any more,' I said. I was trying to make her feel better – although I knew that we could all remember what happened in the classroom.

'Oh, I really hope that is not true, Jessie.' Which took me back a bit. She carried on, 'It is a very sad part of my country's past, but I don't want anyone to forget it. Something like that could happen in this country, you know. Not just Germany.'

She smiled at us and walked off, but I felt a bit rubbish. Actually, I thought it was really rude of her to talk to an English person like that – the whole point was that Nazism happened in Germany, not in England. It was a bit much for her to say it could happen here. We were the ones who fought it, after all.

❧

After school Ben and Yasmin and Kate came back my house – well, Gran's house. Dad opened the door and Snowy charged out.

'I've got him!' said Yasmin, grabbing Snowy, who wriggled with delight in her arms and licked her and wagged his tail madly.

'Thanks, Yasmin,' I said. 'Sorry about all the licking.' Yasmin laughed and put Snowy down, but he obviously decided she was someone he wanted to impress. He kept wagging his tail and bringing toys to her and making big puppy eyes. I was a little bit jealous, but Yasmin loved him so much that I tried not to be.

'He's so sweet!' Yasmin laughed, and made a fuss of him. She was normally so serious it was a bit of a shock to see her as an ordinary girl like me who laughed at puppies and cuddled them. For the first time, I wondered if she had had pets in her country, and if she missed them.

'Try some apple cake before you go to Rose Lodge,' said Mum, carrying in a tray with glasses of lemonade and slices of cake on a plate for us. 'It's Jessie's Gran's recipe.'

I didn't take a slice. I knew Mum was trying to be positive, but I didn't feel like it. I didn't want to eat apple cake ever again if Gran hadn't made it.

'Yummy! It's like the cake Fraulein Bonhoeffer gave us at the end of last term,' said Kate to me. 'I knew it reminded me of something.'

I didn't really want to think about Fraulein Bonhoeffer either, but I was glad Kate was talking to me normally again.

'Sorry about that stuff with Fran,' I said to Kate, collecting up our glasses to take into the kitchen. It was easier to talk about it if I was busy. I didn't have to look at her face. Yasmin and Ben were making a fuss of Snowy.

'It's OK. It's not your fault. Sorry I was so snappy. You were only being nice. I was just fed up.'

'I know,' I said, turning to look at Kate. 'Fran was awful.'

'Yeah, but what's new?' Kate said, shrugging her shoulders and smiling, and this time I didn't try to stick up for my horrible cousin.

❧

Rose Lodge was fun.

Mrs Brady had given us what she called 'memory triggers' for us to use in our oral history interviews – things like cards with pictures of film stars and things from the 1930s and 40s, and even replica board games from the 1940s. They were brilliant. We found out that one lady had a little brother whose gas mask had Mickey Mouse on it, which she was jealous about because her gas mask was just plain. And apparently gas masks smelt awful. The lady, Edna, loved seeing the replica of the original box from a snakes and ladders game, and said her dad had bought her one exactly the same. They had all played lots of board games during the night when there were air raids. We had a silly game of snakes and ladders, with outrageous cheating going on from one of the other ladies, Kathleen, and a man called Bill, who had been evacuated to Canada during the war. It was so interesting. Much better than stupid films about Hitler.

Kate's mum came to collect us, but I said I'd walk back and pop into Mr Gupta's corner shop on the way.

I'd noticed he'd started stocking dog chews, and I thought that might distract Snowy from chewing the house up. The evening had cheered me up, and when I rang Mum to say I was on my way home, I set off in a much better mood. I didn't expect anything bad to happen. It wasn't like I was walking into a wood with a wolf about . . .

Chapter Thirteen

In the queue at Mr Gupta's someone was taking ages over buying a lottery ticket, and then another man tried to buy some beer, but Mr Gupta said he had drunk too much and he couldn't serve him. When he left the shop people in the queue started talking about him and how he was one of the foreign farm workers and nothing but trouble. Normally I would have just listened and thought how much I wanted them to go away too, but I remembered the man at the bus stop who had helped me and Neil. He wasn't like that.

I didn't really want to listen to people talking about the foreign workers any more, and the headlines of the unsold papers Mrs Gupta was taking off the stands looked as depressing as usual, so I read the covers of the fashion magazines, which were much more cheerful – there was a coat on the cover of one that I liked the look of. I was getting nearer the till and next to the bit with the property magazines, and I was imagining buying a whole Scottish castle, when suddenly there was a crash and something came through one of the shop windows at the front. Then there was broken glass all over the top of the freezer and a brick and more bits of glass all over the floor.

'I'm calling the police!' said Mr Gupta. I didn't know what to do. I was second in the queue with the dog chews, and I just stood there feeling sick while he spoke on his mobile phone.

'Don't be frightened, the police will get them,' said Mr Gupta to me and the woman in front, after he put down the phone.

I paid for the dog chews. Mr Gupta's wife started sweeping up the broken glass and people were pointing out where the shards had gone. A police car drew up, its lights flashing, and the two policemen came in, and Mr Gupta started telling them what had happened and about refusing to sell a farm worker more beer earlier. My legs felt wobbly and I had to sit down on the bench outside the shop for a bit before I started walking home. How was something hateful like this happening in our lovely village?

A car pulled up alongside me, and for a minute, hearing it slow down, I felt scared.

'Jess! Jump in!'

It was our car, and it was Mum. 'I've just been to the bottle bank and I was looking out for you on the way back. Why are there police outside Mr Gupta's?'

I fastened my seatbelt and had just told her about the brick coming through the window when I heard Mum exclaim under her breath and slow the car down.

'What is Fran doing here at this time?' She drove up past Fran, who was walking along, her head down.

'Why aren't you at home, Fran?' said Mum, stopping and opening the driver's window. Fran came over. Her face was all streaked with mascara.

'Oh no – what's happened, darling?' said Mum. 'Get in and we'll drive you home.'

Fran got in the back. She looked awful. I could see Mum looking in the mirror, really concerned.

Fran burst into tears.

'Charlie's dead and Mum is so cross with me for going with Dad this weekend. I don't want to go home.'

Charlie was dead! He was such a sweet old dog. I couldn't imagine Aunt Tess's house without him and my eyes felt hot, like I might cry, when I thought about it.

'Oh, love,' said Mum. 'Your mum phoned me about that today. Poor old Charlie. He was in such pain though, Fran. You wouldn't want him to keep suffering.'

'But I loved him. And I didn't even get to say goodbye. Mum put him down today before I got home. I hate her. She wanted to punish me for going with Dad.'

'Fran, love. I know she was hurt, but she'd never do

that. The vet said Charlie was in so much pain that it was kinder to let him go. And she said she tried to ring your mobile last night to get you to come home so you could see him before school, but you had switched it off, and your dad wasn't answering either. They couldn't leave him in agony.'

'I don't want to go home. I don't want to see her. All she does is shout at me and cry. And now Charlie's not even there. He was the only good thing about home.' Fran sniffed – she looked really upset.

'Look, Fran, let's go back to Gran's house together and I'll ring your mum. She's probably worried you're not home yet. Have you got your mobile phone on?'

'No, I didn't want her ringing me and going on again about Dad and his stupid girlfriend. It's not my fault he ran off with her. I don't even like his girlfriend. She hardly even talked to me this weekend. Dad ignored me and Grandad just talked to her. I hate everything. The only person who really loved me was Charlie and he's gone now.'

She was really sobbing now. No one at school would have recognised super cool Fran. I remembered lovely Charlie – how he wagged his tail and loved everyone – and I felt so sorry for her suddenly. And then I remembered her laughing with Nicola Barker and Danny and Liam, I remembered how they'd pushed Neil, and the broken flower pots lying on the ground. I remembered her being so mean to Kate. And I didn't know what to feel. I was glad I was sitting in the front of the car, and not next to her.

When we got back to Gran's, Snowy rushed up to Fran and made such a fuss of her that I don't think anyone noticed that I wasn't rushing to hug her. Fran held him in her arms and he put his paws on her shoulders and tried to lick her tears away.

'He's gorgeous,' she said.

'Well, you would have seen him if you had come back with us last Thursday,' I said.

It must have come out sharper than I meant, because Mum looked over at me and frowned. Fran just kept her head down, hugging Snowy.

'I'm sure Fran had a good reason not to come, Jess, and it's not what she needs to discuss now. Poor Fran has had a shock. Can you make her some hot chocolate?' She beckoned me to come with her into the kitchen, leaving Fran with Snowy in the sitting room.

'Jess, what's the matter with you?' Mum hissed as she picked up the phone to ring Aunty Tess. 'Be nice to your cousin.'

Before I had a chance to answer and point out that I had actually been in a shop when a brick was thrown through the window, Mum was talking to Aunty Tess and walking out into the hall to have a private, one-mum-to-another talk.

I timed it just right so that Mum walked in just as I brought the hot chocolate. It looked like I had taken a lot of trouble making it, as it had loads of marshmallows and a chocolate flake and swirls of cream on the top, but really I'd spent the time in the kitchen adding toppings to avoid being on my own with Fran. Still, it did the trick because Mum and Fran looked so pleased when I brought it in. Snowy sat next to Fran on the sofa and put his head on her knee. She smiled for the first time that evening.

'Your mum is ever so tired,' said mine to Fran, 'so I said how about letting you stay the night here. Have you got the school books you need? I can write a note for your teacher if there's any problem.'

Fran nodded. Her eyes looked extra bright after all that crying.

'Right, that's decided. I'll make up the bed in the spare bedroom. You can go into school with Jessie in the morning.'

Oh no. I couldn't avoid talking to her if she stayed the night. I was going to have to tell her I knew about what she and her friends had done to Neil. I couldn't just ignore it.

Luckily Dad came back then from the hospital and we all had dinner together, so Fran and I couldn't talk on our own anyway. Dad was shocked to hear about the window smashing at Mr Gupta's.

'People said it was the farm workers,' I said.

'How do you know it was them?' said Dad.

'Well, someone said they heard them call out before the brick came through.'

'I don't know, Jessie,' said Dad. 'That's hardly definitive proof. I don't like this blaming the foreign workers for everything. I'm a foreign worker myself – I wouldn't like the French saying the things about me that people here say about the farm workers.'

'But you're not like them, Dad. You don't hang around in bus stops. They talk in their language all the time. No one can understand them. And one of them was drunk.' I felt all my old annoyances bubbling up again – that one man might have been nice, but what about the rest of them?

Dad sighed. 'And you don't think the British get drunk? And as for speaking their language – what do you think English is in France, Jessie? I struggle with my French a lot more than some of those workers struggle with their English. I'm just lucky that a lot of the French speak and understand English. And, believe me, I would hang around in bus stops if I had nowhere else to go and I could meet other English people. It gets really lonely. It makes you look differently at things once you have to go abroad yourself to get work.' For a moment, Dad looked sad. 'I've missed you and Mum so much.'

Poor Dad. He didn't normally say anything about feeling down or lonely.

I looked over at Fran, but she just kept her head down eating her dinner.

As soon as we finished dinner Fran was back on the sofa cuddling Snowy and I managed to avoid her by offering to make the tea. I wished I was the one cuddling Snowy. It was nice that he was so friendly, but it felt a bit disloyal – although how could he know I was annoyed with Fran when no one else did? He's a dog, not a mind reader.

'Thanks love,' said Dad, taking his mug from me. 'Your gran is very worried about that little chap.' He nodded his head over at Snowy. 'She keeps asking if he's safe. I think she's probably still feeling shocked from the fall and that's making her anxious. She'll feel better when she's home. The hospital are hoping to discharge her tomorrow, as long as her blood pressure comes down. The infection seems to have cleared.'

At least that was some good news anyway.

'Aah, look at Fran, poor pet,' said Mum. Fran and Snowy had fallen fast asleep, curled up together, Fran's golden hair on Snowy's white fur. 'She's had a hard time with her dad running off like that and now poor Charlie dying.'

I didn't say anything. All I could think of when I looked at her was the smashed flowerpots and Neil trying not to cry. And him pointing at her and Nicola and Danny and Liam.

I managed to go upstairs with Mum and Fran and say goodnight without being alone with her. I was glad we didn't have to share a room.

I read a bit and then went to the bathroom just before I went to sleep. I hovered outside Fran's door and thought about knocking and going in and telling her I knew all about who had pushed Neil, but when I heard her crying, I didn't.

Chapter Fourteen

Mrs Brady was in the classroom, with 'exciting news'. With Mrs Brady that always means something to do with History, not winning the lottery or having a holiday.

'Well, today we are off timetable all morning for our Second World War project, as we've been given a wonderful and rare opportunity to hear from a very special person.'

Off timetable. On the plus side, that meant no P.E., and no Maths. On the minus side it meant no English and yet *more* History. And I'd had enough of it. I didn't want to hear any more about the Second World War. Not today. It was too gloomy. I'd come to school to stop feeling sad and worried. I wished I was at home with Snowy and Mum and Dad. And Gran. And who was Mrs Brady going to bring on as the 'very special person'?

'I bet it's just Mrs Rowlands with some apples,' whispered Kate.

'Yeah,' I whispered, but I couldn't look at her. I didn't wanted to cry yet again in class.

'Hey,' she said. She put her hand on my arm and gave me an 'Are you all right?' look.

I scribbled: *Sorry Kate. Have to keep on looking ahead or I'll burst into tears. Some horrible things have been happening.*

OK Kate scribbled back, and I heard the snap of chocolate and a rip of paper from under her desk before some silver-wrapped chocolate triangles appeared on my lap. Kate is the best friend ever.

'The person who is talking to us is actually the grandmother of a student here.'

For a weird moment, I panicked it was Gran, and then I saw Ben walk in carrying a laptop, followed by his mum and a small, elderly, grey-haired lady.

They set up the laptop so that we would be able to see slides as Ben's gran talked, and then she began in a soft American voice.

'Good morning. I would like to introduce myself. My name is Miriam MacDonald, but I was born Miriam Levy, a German Jew, in Bavaria, in 1931. And I am a survivor of a concentration camp.'

Then the photos appeared on the screen. But not of barbed wire and high walls, or of starving people. These were happy, family photos, all in black and white, showing two smiling girls and their parents.

112

'My father was a professor of veterinary science. My mother stayed at home to look after my older sister and me. We had a lovely house and a big garden, and life was good. The only sadness I remember from then was when my big sister fell in love and married and emigrated to America, but even then we had big plans to visit her one day. And I still had my family, friends and our dog to keep me company.

'But soon after my big sister Hannah left for America the Nazis came to power and my father lost his job, because he was a Jew. And things were difficult, but because he was so well loved, and because my mother was not a Jew, one of his university colleagues helped us find a place to live in a suburb of Munich. My mother got some secretarial work, and we managed. When I was seven I had to leave school, because I was a Jew, so my father taught me at home, while we hoped and prayed that the Nazis would leave.

'At least at home I could spend more time with my dog Wolfie, whom I loved. I took lots of pictures of him and sent them to my sister in America.'

She put up on the screen a picture of a little white puppy, who looked exactly like Snowy. Everyone went, 'Aaah'.

'Are you sure this is about concentration camps?' whispered Kate. 'I don't get it.'

There were lots of photographs of an adorable little

white puppy. You could tell his owners really loved him, as there were so many of them. He was being held in people's arms, chasing balls, sleeping. There was even a slide of a child's painting of him.

'I did that one,' said Ben's grandmother, smiling. 'Look – there's my name in the corner – Miriam Levy.

'My father said that owning Wolfie was part of his resistance to the Nazis, because the Nazis said that only dark-coloured shepherd dogs, the ones that looked like wolves, were true German Shepherd dogs. And my father did not agree with the Nazis. He said that it didn't matter what colour a dog was, it was what it did – being a German shepherd's dog – that mattered.

'My father's friend showed him a children's book making fun of dogs with different breeds. The Jewish Library has a copy of it.'

She showed us a picture of a book with a strange-looking dog on the cover.

'This is a poodle-pug-dachshund-pinscher. A mongrel dog. Because the Nazis didn't like mongrels. They were only interested in pure breeds. And the book writes about lots of animals that people didn't like – hyenas, locusts, bedbugs, starlings, poisonous snakes, tapeworms and bacteria. Do you know who the writer says all these animals remind him of?'

Nobody said anything.

'The writer says, in this book for little children, that

all these animals, these stupid, or ugly, or lazy, or dangerous animals remind him of Jews. And what do you do with bacteria, or tapeworms, or locusts?'

Kate put up her hand. 'You kill them?'

'Yes,' said Ben's grandmother. 'You kill them. This was a children's book in 1940, in German schools, for little children, and it said that Jews should be killed like vermin. This is what little children were being told to think, even before it was an official law.

'And in the schools, in Maths lessons, the lessons were quite different from the ones you have. The children were being taught to add up how much things cost. That's a good idea isn't it? I mean, I would like my grandson Ben to be more careful with his money.'

She smiled at him and it was a relief to laugh a little as he pretended to be offended.

'But do you know what costs they were worried about? So worried that nearly every day the children did sums about it? Every day at school they were working out how much disabled people, elderly people, sick people, cost the German people to keep in hospital and in care homes. As if disabled people, elderly people, sick people weren't true Germans. And they did sums about how much people cost who didn't work, even though they told my father, and everyone else who was a Jew, that they weren't allowed to.'

I remembered the newspaper headlines in Mr Gupta's.

'When my father saw the maths books, he said we should pray for our lives and I was glad I was learning my maths from him, and not in school any more.

'Then we heard strange, confusing things from my father's friend. That the Nazis had a college for pure-bred dogs because they thought such dogs were so intelligent that they could learn to talk. That the Nazis wanted to ban hunting because it was cruel. Even that Hitler was a vegetarian.'

That was odd. Gran said she had a cousin who worked in a college which taught dogs to speak. So it *was* true. Maybe it was a something all countries did in the war?

'But then we also heard that people's elderly or sick or disabled relatives were disappearing and nobody knew where they were going. My father said that he wished he had taken us to Palestine years before, when the Nazis had first told him to go, or to America with my sister, but he hadn't wanted to leave Germany because he was German and he loved his country. He loved its nature, its stories, its culture, its music. He prayed each day the Nazis would lose power, he stroked our white wolf dog, and he taught me the things I would need to know if I was to grow up to be a vet, but more importantly, to be a good person.

'And then, in 1943, a law was passed that finally broke my father's heart.'

Ben's gran paused, looking out at every single one of us.

'It said that all Jews had to bring their pets to a particular place near where they lived, and that the pets would be killed. That the Jews could not give these pets away, and no non-Jews could accept them. And if they didn't do this, then they and their families would be breaking the law, and would be sent to prison.

'We looked out of the window, and we saw people crying as they walked along the street, carrying cat boxes and cages and little dogs, all on their way to have them put down. For no good reason, except that the Nazis hated us, and wanted to hurt us.

'My father had to take our dog to be shot. Our lovely, beautiful, funny, Wolfie. Who had done nothing. Who loved everyone and whom everyone loved. The most beautiful dog in the world. Whose only crime was to be owned by Jews.'

She stopped. Nobody said anything. She put up a slide of her dog and sat down.

And waited for a few minutes.

And then she got up again.

'Now I am going to tell you what had already happened, and what would happen, to the humans,' she said.

Chapter Fifteen

Lots of us were crying. I could see Fran was really sobbing. I felt sick. I couldn't get the images of those starving prisoners out of my head.

Mrs Levy told us that the first groups of people the Nazis killed were the elderly and the disabled. Old people like Gran and Edna and Kathleen. Old people at home, in hospitals and in residential homes like Rose Lodge, just because they were confused and needed help and the government said this was a waste of money and time. Disabled people. As soon as a baby was born with anything wrong with them their details were sent away and someone marked an 'X' on their form. Kate, my funny, clever, gifted best friend, would have been killed, just because her legs didn't work. Lovely Neil would have been killed because he had Down's syndrome. People's friends and parents and brothers and sisters and children were taken away in buses with tinted windows. Their families were told not to ask about how their relatives died or they would be sent to prison or a concentration camp. The children were given lethal injections or starved to death. If any doctors or nurses told anyone what was happening they would be killed too.

The Nazis sent anyone who disagreed with the government – politicians, priests preaching sermons in church, or even a shopkeeper heard criticising Hitler to his customers – to concentration camps. People who were gay. Communists. Jehovah's Witnesses. Gypsies – Romany people and Sinta people. And most of all, Jewish people. Millions dead because of the Nazis. Millions and millions of them. How could the world have let that happen?

'Listen to me,' Mrs Levy said, as we looked at her last slide of concentration camp victims, shaven-headed skeletons, reaching out their arms to the American army who had come to liberate them. 'This is very important. The point of my story is to warn us not to repeat what happened before. You're a new generation – you're not responsible for what happened in the past, but you are responsible for the future. I want to end this lesson with a story to give you hope.'

We all sat in stunned silence. What could follow any of that?

'So,' Mrs Levy continued, 'the war was eventually won, the concentration camps were liberated, and the world was shocked at the suffering that had gone on. As you have been today. My lovely father, along with millions of others, had died in a concentration camp.' Even though it had happened so long ago, Mrs Levy's clear voice faltered for the first time. She paused for a moment and then carried on. 'My mother and I had nearly died but, somehow, we survived. And we eventually found ourselves back in Bavaria, in the house where we had last lived. And all I could think of was how much I hated them. How much I hated my country, Germany. How my father was wrong to have had hope in its culture and history and to love its mountains, its forests, its lakes and fairy tale castles.

'Every night I had nightmares about what I had seen and would wake up screaming. Every single night.

'Then, one evening, a few months after we returned, when we were still ill and sad and poor and missing my father, there was a knock at the door. There was a girl, about my age. And she had somebody with her – somebody I thought I would never see again.'

She put up the slide of the white dog.

It was Wolfie.

'The girl said that one day, back in 1943, her father had been the vet in charge that day of putting all the Jewish pets down. She said he had hated it, but was scared for his family if he refused. So he tried to organise it so that the pets were killed as quickly and humanely he could. That was all he could do. But then, at the end of a day of killing, he saw his own old professor – the man who had helped him become a vet in the first place. His professor was a Jew and had brought his dog to be put down. The girl said her father could not bear it. He pretended he needed that one dog for experimental war work. But really he brought the dog back to their family farm and hid him. Shortly afterwards he went off to war and was killed, but before he left he made his family promise to keep the dog safe and return it to his old professor if things changed.

'This girl had heard from our neighbours, her relatives, that the Jewish professor's family had returned. So she had walked all the way from a village just outside the town of Dachau, where she lived, to bring Wolfie back to us, even though you could tell she loved him with her whole heart.

'It was so wonderful to see him again. I cannot tell you! And he was so happy to see us. That night he slept on my bed. And each night after that the nightmares got fewer and fewer. It was like, over time, he drove the bad dreams away. Like he was some magic dog.

'It started a whole new time for us. My mother met an American soldier who admired Wolfie when we were out for a walk with him. They fell in love and married. And my new step father brought us all, Wolfie included, back to America with him and we were reunited with my sister and her husband and family. That's where I trained to be a vet myself, met my husband, and had my beautiful daughter, who also became a vet and a dog trainer. Then she had my handsome grandson, Ben, who may become a vet. No pressure, Ben.'

Ben laughed a bit shyly.

'I became a breeder of white German Shepherd dogs, in honour of my father, who I had never forgotten, and Wolfie, my brave and loyal friend who gave us hope.'

Somebody started clapping, but Mrs Levy put up her hand for silence.

'I have often wished I could go back in time, find that German girl and tell her how much her family saving Wolfie meant to me, because I didn't on that day. She kept saying that she was sorry. Over and over again she said that they hadn't known what was happening. Now, when everyone could see what had happened inside Dachau concentration camp, she had finally realised how evil the Nazis were.

'The more she cried and said "sorry", the angrier I got. I told her that she must have known all those years, that people had seen starving prisoners being marched into towns to do slave labour, that they weren't blind. I said I hated her, and I wanted her to rot in Hell. I didn't want to know anything about her – her name, her Nazi vet father, anything. I told her there was no point in saving a dog and letting people die. I would never forgive her and I hoped she would never forgive herself. She ran off weeping, with my curses in her ears.'

I thought Ben's mum was fierce, but I bet that was nothing compared to his gran when she was younger.

'Now, I think that I was wrong. It is only by forgiveness that we can move forwards. I think that girl would indeed have seen the starving Dachau prisoners as they were marched through the streets. But she had been in the system all her life, taught that certain people were good and certain people were bad. The Nazis began by telling the people that the prisoners in Dachau, the very first concentration camp they opened, were all thieves and murderers – people who wanted to hurt them. It was easier to believe this than challenge the Nazis – it is always easier to believe authority than challenge it. I also think, that by the time the townspeople realised this was not true, they had little chance to do anything. Dachau became the place anyone who disagreed with the Nazis – their political prisoners – were sent to. The town butcher was sent there just for saying he did not like Hitler. I have found out that a woman who just gave a sandwich to a prisoner was arrested. I am grateful to those people who did stand up to the Nazis. They did the right thing. But I don't know, if I had been in their position, would *I* have been as brave? Would you?'

I remembered Neil crying over the broken flowerpots at the bus stop, and me not even challenging Fran, Nicola, Danny and Liam, who weren't even Nazi guards, and I knew then that I wouldn't have been.

'It has taken me a lifetime to realise this, but for that girl even to do one thing that went against the system – even such a small thing as hide a dog – that was brave. I had been educated by a wise, humane man, instead of being brainwashed, and I had nothing to be ashamed of. After many, many years, I now can pity her for her shame, and instead of despising her, I would thank her for the courage she had, however little it was.

'So I would like to end by begging you to look out for any early signs of prejudice, any racism, any homophobia, any discrimination against people for their religion – or lack of it, any valuing of people purely for their economic worth, any cruel jokes against the elderly, or the disabled.

'Stop them early, the moment they show their heads, so that those ideas do not take root and take over your country the way they rotted my beautiful Germany. If the attitudes of Nazism hadn't been tolerated in its early stages in the 1930s, those millions of people would never have been murdered.'

I think we must have all looked really shocked, because Ben's gran then said, 'Please, do not despair. Do not think that kindness is worthless, or that because you cannot do everything, you should do nothing. If that girl's father had not taken a risk by saving a dog, my mother and I would never have got our magical Wolfie back at the lowest time of our lives. My mother would never have met the man who became my stepfather, and I would never have had the good life and the lovely family I have had since then.'

We clapped and clapped her and Mrs Brady said we could go outside and have an extra long break after a very challenging morning.

'That was amazing,' said Kate, as we sat by the orchard. She had been crying too, but you could see she was really fired up to fight Nazis, not exhausted by it like me. I sighed and she looked at me. 'What were you going to tell me before the lesson, Jessie. What horrible things have happened?'

I really wanted to tell her, but I suddenly realised I had someone else I had to talk to first.

And then my mobile rang. It was Mum.

'Jessie. Could you get Fran? We've to come and take you to the hospital. Gran is very ill and insisting on seeing you both, and the doctors say we should bring you in as soon as possible. See you in ten minutes at reception.'

Chapter Sixteen

Fran was with Lucy Banks in the girls' loos, fixing her makeup. At least they had both been crying. I couldn't imagine Nicola Barker getting upset after that talk. She wasn't even in school today. I hoped she was off sick. It would serve her right.

'What do you want, Jess?' Fran said. She was trying to be cool Fran again, but she wasn't managing very well and I was in no mood to be patronised.

'Gran's really ill and Mum and Dad are coming to get us to bring us to the hospital. And I need to talk to you on your own, Fran,' I said. Fran stared at me but didn't argue. She picked up her bag and followed me out into the corridor. There were too many people around so I took her straight out into the special courtyard garden for people who were upset. If anyone asked me what we were doing there I'd explain about Gran, but first I had to get something else out of the way.

'I know what you did to Neil.'

'It wasn't me . . .' She didn't even ask what I meant. 'I didn't know they were going to push him over. The shop window wasn't me either. That was the others.'

What?

'So it wasn't the farm workers? It was Liam and Danny and Nicola who threw the brick through Mr Gupta's window?' I said. And even though I thought it should be hard to believe what I was saying, it really wasn't.

'Liam said he was fed up with Mr Gupta because he wouldn't sell him cigarettes.' Fran's voice was quiet and I wondered if she'd been smoking too. 'Liam hates the farm workers too, always hanging around the village and getting in the way. He said let's go and throw a brick in the window and shout something that sounded Polish so we'd get Mr Gupta back and people would think it was the farm workers. He made a joke about killing two foreign birds with one brick, but I didn't want to do it. Not after Neil.'

'So you *did* push Neil over at the bus stop and laugh at him?'

'I didn't. Well, I mean I was with Nicola and Danny and Liam, and they pushed him over, but I didn't. Honestly I didn't, Jess.'

Fran looked at me then and I realised she was ashamed.

'But you didn't stop to pick him up, did you? He was so upset.'

'I couldn't. I couldn't because they had just pushed

127

him. They said he was weird and they expected me to think it was funny.'

'You *did* think it was funny,' I shouted. 'I saw you laughing with them! As I was helping him pick up the flower pots *you* broke.'

Fran went bright red.

'Please, please don't tell Mum, Jessie. She will be so angry with me. I'm sorry. I knew it was wrong but I had to laugh when they were laughing. When I found out they were going to the shop to make trouble, I knew it was wrong so I said I had to go to my cousin's for dinner. I wasn't there when it happened, but I was too scared to say I didn't want to do it.'

'What had you to be scared about? You're the coolest girl in the year. You could have stopped them.'

'I couldn't, Jess. You don't know what they're like – I don't know what to do.'

I stared at her.

'Please, Jessie. Please don't tell Mum.'

'I have to, Fran. If you don't tell her I will. You have to tell her. Today.'

'Can't we wait until Gran's better? Everything is so horrible already.'

I nearly said yes. But then I remembered Neil's face and the way his hands shook. He had been so shocked and scared. And I remembered the sound of the glass, and the shards on Mrs Gupta's clean shop floor, and the way *her* hands shook as she patiently swept them up. And I wanted it to end.

'I'm going to tell Mum and Dad if you don't,' I said. 'They'll be here in five minutes to take us to the hospital to see Gran. She wants to see us.'

'Why, what's the matter with her?' said Fran. 'Why are we going to the hospital in the middle of the day? Is she very ill?' She started crying. 'I'm really sorry, Jessie. I'm sorry about everything. I hate it all. I hate Dad going off and Mum crying all the time and having to change schools because she wanted me home with her. Please don't tell anyone. I just wanted friends.'

'But me and Kate tried to be friendly to you and you just ignored us,' I said. I hadn't realised how angry and hurt I still was about that.

'I know. I'm sorry. I just . . . I just wanted to be cool. I've never been uncool.'

'Like us, you mean?' I think that was the moment I knew I would never look up to Fran any more. 'You didn't want to be uncool? So you chose to ignore us and be friends with people who bully Neil and smash Mr Gupta's window? How cool is that?!'

'I'm really sorry, Jess. You were so nice to me last night with that hot chocolate. I was so sorry then, but I didn't know what to do.'

I thought of Ben's gran telling us about the girl on her doorstep crying and saying how sorry she was and I

129

remembered hovering outside Fran's door last night and hearing her crying herself to sleep. And I remembered how I felt when I saw Danny and Liam and Nicola and Fran coming out of the shop. And that I hadn't told anyone that I knew who had pushed Neil over. I wasn't that brave either.

I got out my mobile phone and checked the time.

'Come on, Fran. Mum and Dad should be waiting at reception for us by now. We'll tell them together.'

Chapter Seventeen

Sometimes, when you are sorry and try to do the right thing in the end, things are still horrible for a while. We couldn't sort anything out straight away because Mum and Dad were so keen to take us to see Gran as soon as possible I knew we couldn't start telling them about Liam and the others until after the visit.

'After the hospital. You've got to tell them,' I quickly said to Fran as their car drew up. She nodded, looking really miserable, but Mum and Dad didn't ask what was the matter because they just thought it was about Gran.

We were *all* miserable about Gran. She was lying in her bed looking so anxious, tossing and turning and muttering in her sleep.

Even though she'd been given something to help her sleep, it didn't seem to be working.

'I wish we knew what she's worrying about,' said Mum. 'She's never going to get better if she doesn't rest properly.'

We waited a bit, but the nurses said it would be a long time before she woke up and they apologised for calling us over. It hadn't been that big an emergency after all.

When we went home, Fran confessed. I thought she was going to avoid it again, but in the end it all came out in a big splurt and she kept saying 'sorry' and crying. I was sorry for her, but I was also a bit fed up. I knew Mum and Dad were really disappointed with me for not telling anyone that I knew who had pushed Neil over and I didn't blame them. The police came round and talked to both of us and Fran had to go off to the station. Dad went with her, as well as Aunty Tess, and Uncle Mark, who'd come from London. Later they went and saw Neil and his mum to say sorry. The community policeman said that there might have to be a court case eventually if the Guptas pressed charges, but Fran probably wouldn't be needed to give evidence.

'What an awful day,' Dad said when he got back.

'I'm so sorry,' I said again. Snowy put his paws on my knees and I lifted him up on to my lap. It was such a comfort to bury my face in his soft white puppy fur.

'Have you got any homework, love?' said Mum. 'And Jessie, you did the right thing in the end.' She gave me a kiss. It was kind of Mum to say that, but I just wished I had a magic spell to turn back time and do things differently – do them better. I didn't like knowing I'd taken so long to do the right thing.

'I've got a fairy tale to read for my English homework,' I said. I'd actually forgotten about that bit of the homework.

'That's nice,' said Mum. 'A fairy tale should cheer you up. You do that then. I'll get on with dinner but I'll make you some hot chocolate now and you can curl up in Gran's armchair and read it.'

So I popped Snowy, now sleeping, in his basket, settled down in Gran's armchair with my hot chocolate and started reading *The Robber Bride*.

It didn't cheer me up AT ALL. It was truly horrible.

Basically, a miller has a beautiful daughter and he arranges a marriage for her with a very rich man. But the girl has a very bad feeling about this man, and isn't really happy about it. So then the man asks her to visit him in his house in the dark forest, and it says:

When Sunday came, and it was time for the girl to start, a feeling of dread came over her which she could not explain, and that she might be able to find her path again, she filled her pockets with peas and lentils to sprinkle on the ground as she went along.

It reminded me a bit of the Hansel and Gretel story, which always made me want to carry white pebbles in my pockets when I was little, in case I got lost and needed to find my way home. I knew breadcrumbs would be useless. I used to really worry about it.

Anyway, this girl walks on into the deepest, darkest part of the forest, where she finds a lonely, grim and mysterious house, which she doesn't like at all.

That made me think of Hansel and Gretel again, except that of course for Hansel and Gretel the evil witch's gingerbread house looked lovely and tasty.

As this girl goes up into the lonely house she hears:

Turn back, turn back, young maiden fair,
Linger not in this murderers' lair

And it turns out that it's a bird in a cage, warning her.

She goes in and finds an old lady, who tells her that she is in a murderers' den and that the man she is to marry plans to kill her there, but the old lady says she will help her. Then there's the revolting bit. The old lady hides her just in time for her to escape the murderous robber crew, who she sees bring in, kill and CHOP UP (!!!) another girl. She hears the other girl pleading for mercy. I nearly stopped reading, particularly when, after they had murdered her, one of them chopped her finger off to get her ring.

This wasn't my idea of a fairy tale. Imagine a Robber Bride ride in Disneyland!

So anyway, the girl escapes with the old lady. They follow the path where the lentils and peas are growing (that was quick . . .) back to the miller, and tell him everything. Then they decide to lay a trap.

The girl goes to get married as arranged, and all the wedding guests are invited to tell a story. The evil robber bridegroom asks the girl to tell a story and so she tells the story of how she went to the wood and found this house, except that after the bird cries out:

Turn back, turn back, young maiden fair.
Linger not in this murderers' lair,

She adds on a bit and tells them all that the bird said:

My darling, this is only a dream.

Which was weird because she knew it was real. The only thing I could think was that maybe telling people it was only a dream was the only way to keep them listening. Maybe if they thought it was real it would be too horrible for them to accept.

Anyway, she carries on and tells the story and in between her telling the gory details you keep hearing the words 'My darling, this is only a dream'. Then she gets to the bit where she sees one of the robbers cutting off the murdered girl's finger and she says:

'But the finger sprang into the air and fell behind the great cask into my lap. And here is the finger with the

ring.' And with these words the bride drew forth the finger and showed it to the assembled guests.

I said 'ugh!' out loud at that, but at the same time another bit of me thought how glad the bride probably was to be able to do something at last about what she had seen. It must have been so horrible when she couldn't do anything to help when the girl was being murdered – at least this time she could make sure justice was done.

And then it finished:

The bridegroom, who during this recital had grown deadly pale, up and tried to escape, but the guests seized him and held him fast. They delivered him up to justice, and he and all his murderous band were condemned to death for their wicked deeds.

Now I had to decide whether it was a happy ending. I wrote:

I think The Robber Bride *has a happy and a sad ending at the same time. The maiden gets justice for the murdered girl by telling her story but this cannot undo the fact that she was murdered in the first place. The severed finger is an image that stays with you long after the story ends and doesn't allow you to forget the*

horrible bit. I do not think this story is suitable for
bedtime or cartoons.

And I scooped Snowy up from his basket, not worrying about waking him up, and gave him an extra big cuddle. Aunty Tess rang after dinner and had a long conversation with Mum and Dad. They told me that she was keeping Fran off school for a few days and she and Uncle Mark and Fran were going to meet up and decide how to help her, as she was so unhappy. Apparently Fran was saying she wanted to go back to her old boarding school and Aunty Tess said it would be good for Fran to get away from the undesirable influences at ours.

'Not that Tess can blame your school for Fran making bad friends,' said Dad. 'She has to let Fran take responsibility for her own actions, or she'll never learn from them. We're proud you're doing that, Jessie.'

It was funny. People were being very nice to me but I still didn't feel that great about what I'd done.

'Another of those postcards from Germany came today,' said Mum, changing the subject as she sat back in her armchair drinking tea. 'You can have it, Jess. Still no clues to who's sending them.'

She took it from the pile of post on the coffee table and passed it to me. This time it was a painting of a wood. I turned it over and it was addressed to Maria Bayer again, this time with a message:

Remember the beautiful countryside.

'It's a pity this Maria is missing out on these cards,' said Mum.

I brought it upstairs when I went to bed, and looked at the wood on the card and thought of how happy I had been with Snowy at the dog class, and how lovely Ben Green was. Then I thought about what his gran had been through and I felt sad again. And then I thought of my own lovely gran still in hospital. Nothing was nicely finished off. There were no real happy endings, and it made me want to cry.

I looked over at Snowy, asleep in his crate. I had asked Mum and Dad if I could have him in my room again, and they said that after all the rough few days I'd had they thought I deserved a treat. Snowy's paws were twitching in his sleep and he was wagging his tail. His dreams must have been happy. He deserved them.

I wished I could do something properly good. I wished I could at least help Gran get better. It was like she'd left all her energy back in the past, when she needed it to get well now.

I took the picture of the girl and her dog from under my pillow and looked at her.

'How can I make it better?' I asked, but obviously, she didn't have the answer any more than I did.

Chapter Eighteen

The next day at school Mr Hunter asked us what we thought of *The Robber Bride*.

'I thought it was horrible,' said Lucy. 'I much prefer *Cinderella* or *Sleeping Beauty*.'

'Why?' asked Mr Hunter.

'They're just nicer. I would never give my children a fairy tale like that. It's just not . . . nice.'

'Lots of people have found problems with the gory violent bits in these stories,' Mr Hunter said. 'Would you have liked that for a bed time story when you were a small child?'

We all shook our heads.

'I wouldn't have been able to sleep after that,' said Lizzie Young.

'What if I told you that there was a man called Bruno Bettelheim who said fairy tales like these could help children?' said Mr Hunter. 'How could that be?'

Yasmin put up her hand. She doesn't talk much in

class, so when she says anything it's a big thing.

'Because life isn't happy and safe. Because bad things do happen to people, and you can't do anything about it sometimes.' That was the most she'd ever said in class. She looked back down at her desk as soon as she said that, and I noticed she kept turning a paper clip over and over in her hand. You could see Mr Hunter had noticed that she was upset, but he didn't want to draw attention to her.

'Excellent, Yasmin!' he said, and kept talking as he walked around the room.

I looked over at Yasmin. Now she was taking out pencils and putting them back in her pencil case and taking them out again as if it was the most important job in the world, as if it was the only thing she could do.

'Bruno Bettelheim was one of many who would have totally agreed with you. He said that fairy tales are not meant to be nice, or sweet and safe, but to help us make sense of a difficult world. He used them with very disturbed children, because he often said you could understand the odd things they did if you could understand the story they were living in. Some people's lives are a bit like disturbing fairy tales – they are living in stories where chairs are not for sitting on, but are used to hit them, or where parents are not kind and loving, but more like wicked witches, and when they are in the "normal" world, with "normal" people, these people

140

don't understand why they are behaving in the way they do. You have to know the story the person is in sometimes before you can change it and bring about a happy ending for everyone. Now, for the rest of the lesson I'd like you to do some more work on the fairy tale you are writing. Yasmin, I wonder if you could spare a few minutes to help me get some books from next door?'

Mr Hunter and Yasmin went out and came back after a while with some books from the library. I'm sure he just wanted to check if she was all right. He really is so lovely. We all got on with our fairy tales. Well, I doodled a few pictures of castles. My mind wasn't on it. I'd been thinking about Gran and I'd realised what I had to do to help her. I couldn't wait for the lesson to end.

Kate was brilliant. As soon as I explained at break about my idea about the box of photographs Snowy had found under Gran's bed and how Gran was stuck in the past apologising for something we didn't know anything about, she waved her magic wand of organisation and sorted it all out, so that at lunch Ben Green came over to the table where Yasmin and Kate and I were having our sandwiches.

'I've just rung Mum and she says it's fine for you all to come back to ours tonight,' said Ben. Kate was a genius. She had grabbed him at the end of break and explained that we had a sort of history mystery to solve and our group should do it – that we had a box of old photos which would help us find out what was upsetting Gran and could me and her and Yasmin come and look at them in his house. He hadn't argued at all, she said. In fact, he seemed quite pleased. Which cheered me up in spite of everything. Not that I was thinking it was because of me, you understand. Just . . . well, that it cheered me up. Which I knew was what Kate meant to do. She knew how much I liked being with Ben. It would be fun to see his house. And it looked like Yasmin was happy with the idea too.

❧

I went home to Gran's first. There was no problem getting Mum and Dad to agree to me going to Ben's, especially when they heard Yasmin and Kate were going to be there.

'Dad,' I said. 'What do you know about Gran's childhood?'

'Well, I know it wasn't happy,' he said, loading up the dishwasher.

'How do you know?' I said.

'Well, your grandad always told me never to ask her about it, and she never said anything.'

'But do you know where she was born, or where she went to school, or anything like that? How did she meet Grandad, for example?'

'That was in London. She was working for an American friend of Grandad – she was a secretary.'

'And do you know if she went camping when she was a child? I mean, she was so good at it. She must have learned it from somewhere. That must have been a happy bit. Did she ever talk about that?'

'Honestly, Jess, I never gave it a thought,' Dad said, putting the washing tablet in and shutting the door firmly. He pressed the button and the dishwasher lights came on. 'My dad was in the army, so maybe he taught her when they were first married. Why do you want to know?'

'I just wondered . . .' It was hard to put my thoughts into words for Dad, who hadn't been there in Mr Hunter's lesson. '. . . Gran keeps saying sorry for something – maybe it's something from her childhood? Maybe she did something wrong?'

'Your *gran*? She's not got any skeletons in the cupboard. She's never done anything wrong in her life. She had an unhappy childhood, that's why she never spoke about it. Can you imagine Gran doing anything wrong? Really, Jess?' He laughed. 'Now, Mum and I are going to the hospital to check up on Gran again and see if the new medicine is working. Are you all right to walk to Ben's and back yourself? Bring the key in case we're late home.'

There was no point talking to Dad about this. I love

143

Dad, but he isn't always very good at listening. I went upstairs, took the photo from under my pillow, put it in my coat pocket and, after checking nobody was about, quickly went into Gran's room. I found the new box where Mum had put it on the top of the wardrobe, stood on a chair to get it down and put it in my rucksack. I didn't feel guilty. I felt Gran wanted me to do it, and I knew I couldn't explain.

'Jessie!' I heard Mum call, but she hadn't caught me. 'I've just rung Ben's mum and asked her if you could bring Snowy with you. Do you mind? He's been left too much on his own today already. She says it's fine.'

I stuffed my pockets with plastic bags and dog treats and took Snowy on the lead to Ben's house. Ben's mum made a big fuss of him and sent Ben's younger twin brothers off with him to play in the garden with their very friendly, waggy dogs. Snowy looked like he'd just been invited to the best party ever. He ran around the garden at top speed with a plastic flowerpot in his mouth and then fell over his feet and looked very surprised before getting up to chase after the big dogs again. Ben's brothers thought it was hilarious and started playing football with him. We sat in the kitchen and Ben's mum got out some juice and biscuits to keep us going. Then I got out the box.

It wasn't exactly what I had imagined. We were sitting around the box on their big kitchen table and most of

Ben's family were there. I didn't mind too much, as I really liked his mum and gran, who said 'how interesting' politely, but were busy making dinner in the background.

'This is like being history detectives,' said Kate. 'Come on, Jess, tip them out. Let's see if we can solve this mystery!'

Chapter Nineteen

We put aside the packet of envelopes, tied with a ribbon, because reading private letters seemed a bit too much, especially as I wasn't supposed to have taken the box in the first place, and we concentrated on looking at all the loose black-and-white photos, like the one of the girl and her dog.

It all looked very happy and normal, whatever Dad said. There were some happy photos of a little blonde girl and an older boy and adults we assumed were their parents. A bit like Mrs Levy's presentation. They seemed to go on a lot of foreign holidays, often camping by lakes or mountains. They had a little Beetle car, which is just the sort of car I've always wanted.

'I wonder if that's a picture of Gran and her family,' I said. 'That would explain why she's so good at camping.'

'No, this girl is called Maria or Sophie,' said Kate, looking at the back. Another Maria, I thought. Funny how it was coming up again. First the card to Maria Bayer and now this. 'Maria, Thomas, Martin and Sophie,' read Kate and she put the photo back on the table.

'Oh. I don't know any of those names . . . Gran's only ever mentioned her cousin Heidi . . .'

'The one with the talking dogs?' Kate said, but I was still thinking about Gran.

I supposed this made sense. 'All these are obviously somewhere foreign and Gran's never left Great Britain. We always teased her about it. She said Scotland was far enough away for her.'

'Here's another one of the children,' Ben said. 'Maria and Thomas – so the girl must be Maria, the boy Thomas, the mother Sophie and the dad Martin. They're in the mountains. It looks like Switzerland or Austria or somewhere.'

We looked through the other photos, but they were all of Maria and Thomas, smiling outside a pretty church with a solemn priest, others of them looking happy in what looked like some sort of scouts uniform, playing games on a field with other children.

'And there's one with an older girl and two Alsatians "Maria and Heidi, Hugo and Karl",' Kate said.

'Wow, it's Heidi!' I said, 'and perhaps those are the dogs she was trying to teach.'

'Aah, look at this one!' said Yasmin, holding up a photo of two girls, about twelve, each with blonde hair and plaits, standing on some grass by a fence in front of a long line of hutches. They were beaming into the camera as they cuddled an extremely fluffy rabbit. She turned it over.

'It says it's of Maria and a girl called Gudrun. Look – it says something . . . I can't read the handwriting very well. It says "D" something something something . . . I think that's a "U" at the end . . . and then 1941.'

Kate got out her phone. 'Pass it to me. I'm going to look it up. That rabbit is seriously cute. Maybe D-whatever is a breed I haven't heard of.' Kate wanted to have a rabbit herself one day, and (typically) had researched it all thoroughly. If she didn't recognise a rabbit breed it must have been rare.

Ben's mum and gran joined us at the table.

'I'm sorry to hear about your grandmother being ill,' said Mrs Levy.

Without warning my eyes filled with tears. My coat was over the back of the chair so I searched in my pocket for a tissue, but my hand brought out the photo of the girl and the dog. The girl, I could now see, was an older, sadder Maria. Also in my hand were the pieces of paper Gran gave to me in the hospital. This was the coat I'd been wearing that day. As usual, I hadn't emptied my pockets.

'In the hospital she kept giving me paper with letters on,' I said, passing one of them to Mrs Levy. 'She wanted me to give them to my friends, especially Kate. She's really upset and I don't know why.'

She took it and looked at the paper with the initials *JM* on.

'Very strange,' she said. 'I wonder what they stand for? Is there someone in your family with those initials, I wonder? Someone she wants to contact?'

'I don't think so. She keeps saying we have to show the paper to people, but I don't know who she's talking about,' I said. 'And we've found all these photos of people I've never seen before.' I passed her the photos we'd looked at.

'It's Dachau,' said Kate, suddenly. She was staring at her phone.

'What?' said Mrs Green.

Dachau . . . ?

'I tapped in "*D* blank blank *ch* blank *u rabbit*" and it suggested "*angora rabbits Dachau*", and look!'

She passed me the photo and her phone with the article up on the screen. It was something I really *really* did not want to see, but I couldn't stop reading.

Angora rabbits, looked after by concentration camp prisoners. Dachau concentration camp.

There was a picture of them by a line of hutches like in the photo, but this time the people holding them were men in stripy uniforms, guarded by Nazi soldiers. They were so thin they looked like skeletons – *skeletal* is the word.

Kate looked over my shoulder and read out loud what the article said. 'It says the Nazis bred angora rabbits because they used the soft fur to line German airforce coats. Himmler, the head of the S.S., who ran the concentration camps, loved them. They were sheared for their fur, not killed, and brushed and combed, and fed and watered. The rabbits lived in clean, airy hutches just outside the very concentration camps where human beings died in terrible conditions.' Kate went pale, then read out word for word, '"Himmler's daughter Gudrun visited Dachau Concentration camp in 1941. She went to the herb garden, met the local vet and his family and enjoyed cuddling the rabbits."' And there, as Kate scrolled down for us to see, was another photo. It was almost exactly the same one Yasmin had found, the one I was holding in my hand. Gudrun, the blonde girl holding the rabbit so tenderly, smiling out at the camera with her friend, Maria, in front of a row of hutches.

'I don't know what it means,' I said, my mind was full of ideas all jumbled up like a jigsaw made of the wrong pieces.

Ben had taken the photos from his Gran and was going through them.

'Look – the handwriting on the back of the photos – Maria, Thomas, Martin and Sophie. It's not "and". It's "und". Maria und Thomas, Maria und Gudrun. Und isn't English. It's German.'

We looked back at the other photos. All the times we thought it had said 'and' it had said 'und'.

Concentration camp. Germany. I felt sick.

There was a long silence, and then Kate said, in a voice that wasn't like her normal one, 'I think I know what your gran's secret is. She must have had cousins or something who were Nazis in Germany. She definitely said to you she had a cousin called Heidi who worked in a college for dogs – and Ben's gran said the Nazis had a college for dogs. Remember?' I didn't dare look at Ben's gran, who had gone very quiet. 'And here is someone called Heidi with a dog. In Germany. In 1940. Nazis bred angora rabbits at Dachau – and here is a photo of Maria and Gudrun with a fluffy angora rabbit in Dachau. In 1941. It's too much of a coincidence,' said Kate. 'Your gran's family were Nazis.'

It was out. And the words couldn't be unsaid. Like some magic incantation.

We looked at each other.

I found myself going red, but it wasn't for the usual reasons. I was sitting at table with a survivor of a concentration camp.

There was a horrible silence around the table.

151

'The Nazis hated the disabled. They took them away and killed them the first of all, even before the Jews,' said Kate slowly, her voice wobbling.

Ben's grandmother had picked up the picture of the girls in scout uniform and was staring at it. She put it next to the sheets of paper with *JM* on them.

'Jungmadel,' she said. 'Your grandmother has photos of Young Maidens.'

'Sorry?' I said.

'The initials "J" and "M". All German Nazi girls had to be members of the Hitler Youth. First they were members of the Young Maidens, or the jungmadel, then, at fourteen they became members of the B.D.M., or Bund Deutscher Madchen. At thirteen you'd be members of the J.M. still.'

'Gran keeps talking about us being young maidens. And buttons. And white blouses.' I was talking to Ben's gran, but looking at the table.

'Yes. The uniform of the girls in the Hitler Youth was a white blouse and a blue skirt, and the buttons were special because, whether they were in the Jungmadel or the Bund Deutscher Madel, they all had the initials B.D.M. on them. It was rather like the Brownies are younger members of the Girl Guides. They wore a black kerchief with a brown leather knot.' She picked up the pictures of the happy, smiling girls. 'Like these girls are wearing.'

152

Young Maidens. Hitler Youth. My gran wanted us to become people who had put fear and misery into the lives of so many millions of people.

My gran wanted us to be Nazis.

Chapter Twenty

'I'm sorry. I want to go home.'

Kate – calm, bossy, organised Kate – was crying. She had wheeled herself away from the table and to the doorway, and had her back to me.

'Please,' she said to Ben's mum. 'Please take me home now. I want to go home. I have to go home.'

I didn't know what to do. I just sat there feeling sick, looking down at the table.

'I'll stay with Jessie,' said Ben's gran.

'OK,' Ben's mum said. I just sat where I was, not looking at Kate, as Ben's mum got her car keys. 'Yasmin, I'll drop you home too, shall I?' I heard her say.

'Ben – you go with your mother,' said his gran. 'I just want to talk to Jessie for a few minutes.' It felt like everything was happening far away.

The door slammed, and everything was silent. I had no words. I knew that Ben's gran was still sitting in the kitchen, but neither of us were moving or saying anything. All I could hear was the ticking of the kitchen clock. A tear rolled down my cheek and plopped on to the table. I heard Mrs Levy get up and open the door into the garden. Suddenly there was a scampering and Snowy and the other dogs erupted into the kitchen. You could hear their panting and the thud of their wagging tails and the scratching of their toe nails on the hard floor. Ben's gran was calling to the twins in the garden, asking them to play outside a while longer. I felt Snowy putting his paws on my knee and I scooped him up. He felt warm and alive, like a huge teddy.

Then I felt Mrs Levy's arm around my shoulder.

'I'm so sorry,' I cried, but it all came out muffled as I was talking into Snowy's fur.

She squeezed my shoulders and gently put her hand under my chin to raise my head. Snowy got in the way and promptly licked my nose, which made us laugh.

'Jessie. You have nothing to apologise for.'

'But . . . I'm so sorry. I can't understand. Why does she want us to be in the Hitler Youth? Why does she want us to be Nazis? I feel so ashamed. After everything you told us.'

I hugged Snowy closer. I felt so bad. Maybe something as evil as Nazism stayed in a family, and that's why Fran had done what she had done. Maybe I was cursed. Maybe my family was cursed.

'Look. I know your friend Kate is very upset,' said

Mrs Levy. 'I understand that. It is a shock to see these photos from Nazi Germany, and to know that they are somehow connected to your grandmother's family. But from what you say, someone talking about papers and staying safe, someone choosing to have a white German Shepherd dog, sounds more like someone who was not doing what the Nazis wanted. I think all this about the Hitler Youth is about some sort of identification, for your protection. All German children had to be in it. A lot of them thought it was fun. They went camping and on trips and sang songs. I honestly think I would have wanted to be in it if I had been old enough when it started – not that Jewish girls were allowed.

'Your Gran's illness seems to have made her think she is back in the 1930s and 40s, the time of these photos. The question is, why would she think she had to protect you from being sent to prison by the Nazis? The Nazis weren't here, although perhaps she was scared they were going to invade Britain . . . and perhaps someone in her family wrote to her about the Nazis shooting white German Shepherd dogs?'

Snowy twisted round and gave my nose another lick and I suddenly felt hopeful again. I couldn't bear thinking that my gran wasn't lovely. She had been kind and loving all my life. I didn't know this new person. It felt like the world was turned inside out. Maybe Ben's grandmother was giving me the chance to turn it back the right way again. Maybe Gran was in the wrong story, doing the right things.

'Jessie – who is this girl?' Mrs Levy's voice had changed. It sounded excited, amazed.

I looked over to see her holding the picture of Maria and the dog in her hands.

'I don't know. It must be her cousin or someone. I found it in the box, and the dog reminded me of Snowy, so I kept it.'

'This is the girl,' she said. 'I thought I recognised her from the other pictures, but I wasn't sure. She was younger and fatter in those – but this is exactly what she was like when I met her – thinner and older and so much sadder.' I wasn't sure what she meant until she said, 'This is my Wolfie. This is my Wolfie when he was given back to us. I can't believe it. Jessie, it can't be a coincidence that your grandmother has this photo. I have thought about the girl who brought Wolfie back for so long, and these past nights I have been dreaming of her. I thought it was just because of my talk . . .'

We stared at each other, fairy tale magic unfolding around us.

'There are some letters too in the box, but I haven't looked at them,' I said. 'Dad and Mum didn't want me to open the box again in the first place, and looking at Gran's private letters seemed worse than looking at her photos, somehow.'

'We could look at the postmarks anyway, I suppose,' said Mrs Levy, taking up the packet and undoing the red ribbon keeping them together. 'These are from Germany. They seem to have been sent from Dachau every year for years – my goodness – there are at least twenty of them. Then this larger one . . . It's been opened. And the postmark is . . .' Mrs Levy looked up at me. 'Jessie. When did your gran get Snowy?'

'Last week.' My voice trembled when I said it.

'This was posted the Wednesday before.' She passed me the envelope.

'I'm not sure I can read that much German,' I said.

'I can,' she replied. Our eyes met. I knew inside me what was right.

I lifted the flap of the envelope and reached inside.

But what was inside wasn't in German, it was in English.

It was a big homemade card. Someone had stuck three postcards on the front. There was a painting of a girl in a forest carrying firewood, followed by a dog, and another of a donkey and a dog standing together. I liked them immediately. They were like impressionist paintings. The third card was an ordinary photographic postcard of a marketplace with a pretty church with a boy and a girl wearing the traditional costumes of Bavaria that Fraulein Bonhoeffer had taught us about – the boy wearing lederhosen and the girl wearing a dirndl dress.

I opened it.

Dear Great Aunt Maria, it started. I felt really disappointed.

'It's not for Gran – it's for a Maria,' I said. 'We keep getting cards addressed to a Maria. It's from the same person. It's just a mistake.'

'Then why did your gran keep it?' said Mrs Levy, quietly. 'Read on.'

'"I know that my grandfather tried very hard to contact you for many years and that although he wrote to you many, many times before he died, you only wrote back once. This is the only address I have for you, so I don't even know if this will ever get to you. I lit a candle in St Jacob's that it would, and something in me thinks it will.

'"I know that you said that you never wanted to speak or to hear German again. I know you were very ill and that you left Germany to get better. I know that you said that now you had an English family now, and an English name. That you were Elizabeth Jones, and would be until you died."'

Maria. Maria and Wolfie. Gran and Snowy. Ben's gran and the weeping girl she would not forgive. I could not speak for a moment. The girl in the photograph was Maria. The girl in the photograph was *Gran.*

'Carry on, Jessie,' said Ben's gran, and reached over to stroke Snowy as I picked up the card again, my hands shaking.

'"But now it is my turn to try",' I continued reading. '"My father was my grandfather's only son, and I was his only granddaughter. I was named after you. I loved my grandfather very much. When he was dying he asked me to try again to find you, and to meet your English family. He said he loved you, and he loved Germany. He said he was so sorry for everything that had happened when he was young, and that he hadn't kept trying to contact you because he didn't want to make you ill again. He wanted me to tell you that he would always love his little sister.

'"So I am writing to you in English, in the hope that you or your family will read this. I am fourteen. I have no cousins in Germany, and I would love to meet my English family. But I would also like my English family to come to Germany, to see that Dachau is a beautiful market town with a wonderful history from before the Nazis ruined it, as they tried to ruin everything. I want you to see how the Camp has become a memorial to honour the dead, and I want you to see the art gallery we have with all the wonderful Dachau art in it – art that shows the beautiful Dachau countryside and the thing that Dachau was famous for before the Nazis. My grandfather said you drew and painted all the time – so do I, and I wonder if I have any cousins who do too?

'"These photos I enclose from your childhood are photos my grandfather asked me to send you. He kept them all his life. I have taken copies of all of them. If you are not Elizabeth Jones or a member of her family, please could you send them back to me. I will pay you. These are very precious.

"'I hope that someone in my family will read this and make contact. Maria Bayer.'"

And then there was an address in Dachau in Germany and a telephone and an email.

Ben's gran reached over and hugged me and Snowy, tears pouring down her face.

❧

A few days later, when it was all over, I told Kate, who was sitting on Gran's sofa cuddling Snowy, how Mrs Levy came to the hospital with me, determined this was why she had met me and Snowy. She went up to my gran's bed and sat down beside her, and she watched as Gran tossed and turned and muttered in her sleep. Then she reached out and took Gran's hand in hers.

'Maria,' she said. 'Maria Bayer. Can you hear me? It is Miriam Levy. Wolfie's owner. You brought him back to me. Thank you. Thank you for keeping my white wolf safe.'

Gran held on to her hand and opened her eyes. She looked at Ben's gran and then turned her head away and I saw tears roll down her cheeks.

'Forgive me,' she said. 'I am so sorry. I am so ashamed.'

'Please,' said Ben's grandmother. 'I understand now. I forgive you. You were only a child.'

'I did nothing to stop them.' Gran's voice was barely a croak.

'What could you do?'

'I don't know. I just wish I had known . . .'

'Wish you had known what?'

'That everything I believed in was wrong. That nothing was beautiful. That it was all rotten at the core. I thought it was so beautiful, the story they told us. Our lovely country. We were the golden people, the good people. I tried so hard to be good. Everything is spoilt, everything is destroyed. And now I am so frightened it is happening again. And I can't stop it.' Her shoulders shook with silent sobs.

'No, it isn't. We won't let it. They don't have the right to destroy everything we loved, everything we love. We know the signs to look out for, and we can stop it this time. That's what I tell the children, Maria, and I believe it. They will not become Nazis. You don't have to fear. Look, Maria. Look.'

And Miriam Levy took the piece of paper I had given her, with the initials my grandmother had drawn on it with so much fear, and ripped it up, from top to bottom and from side to side, until it was in tiny pieces, like snow or confetti. And my grandmother watched her until the pieces were scattered over the floor, and she looked into Miriam Levy's face as if to check whether what she was saying was really true.

The next minute they had their arms around each other, and they were both crying and crying as if they could never cry enough.

Much later, Mrs Levy still sat beside my gran, holding her hand, until she finally fell asleep.

Jessie Jones 9B
Mr Hunter, English.

Write a Modern Fairy Tale

A warning about fairy tales . . .

Once upon a time there was a girl called Maria who lived in a beautiful fairy-tale land.

You wouldn't think it looking at her when she was old, but, growing up, she had golden hair. That was good in her particular fairy tale. Everyone said so. Her mother had golden hair too, and she loved to watch her brush it in the evening.

And her eyes were blue. Really blue. Her skin pale, but her body strong. She could run and climb and swim too. And sing. And paint beautiful pictures of her beautiful fairy-tale town. She had a beautiful voice even as a little child. She worked hard and she was honest and brave and kind.

At least, she tried to be. She really wanted to be good.

She wanted to be happy, to be free. She wanted not to have to worry about her enemies.

Because, like in all fairy tales, the goodies had enemies.

You may have some yourself.

Maybe no one you actually know, just people you read about in the newspapers who unfairly pretend to be poor, but really they are just lazy and stay in bed while your family have to go to work. Or maybe people you hear about who come from far away to take jobs so that your own father or mother, brother or sister, can't have one. People in magazine articles who lie and cheat to get money they don't deserve. People who pretend they are ill and then someone sees them go skipping down the street. Fraudsters, scammers, scroungers. Baddies.

Those were Maria's enemies. She had never actually met any, but her leader told her all about them and how bad they were. He told how her own father and mother had once been very poor because of them.

Maria was happy because she had a leader who promised her that he would get rid of all their enemies, and her family believed him because he was a very brave man, who had been in the army, and who loved painting and babies and animals. Her mother had a picture of him holding a baby deer. He banned hunting, because he said it was cruel, and Maria was proud she had such a good man to lead her country.

And her leader worked very hard. Such a lonely, brave man. An artist. He wanted his people to have families, to have room to live, to be happy, but he had no time himself to meet anyone. Some of the girls Maria knew imagined marrying him. They sent him photographs and letters telling him so.

Anyway, with such a leader, Maria could feel truly safe in her beautiful country, and relax and get on with the rest of her life.

At least, that's what she thought.

In her wonderful fairy tale.

Before it all went wrong. Before the marching began, and people began being killed, just for being different, or ill, or not agreeing with their leader.

Who wasn't so wise and wonderful after all.

Who took her lovely fairy-tale country and made it into a nightmare. An unspeakable nightmare. For years and years and years.

And the people he said were the enemies weren't the real baddies at all – it was the people he said were the good people who were the real enemies.

In her beautiful fairy-tale land.

Maria had to watch while people starved to death in the streets in front of her, and others disappeared and never came back. And she was very scared. She knew that if she tried to do the smallest good thing she would disappear too.

That was when she realised that she wasn't that brave after all.

Millions of innocent people suffered and died because of the story they were living in, that was being told, the story Maria listened to, her fairy tale.

And now I am worried about the fairy tales we are told today. That it's not once upon a time but Now. I am worried that in our world there are Goodies and Baddies and a story that is being told that we believe in, just like Maria believed in hers.

But we have not checked who is telling it.

I had to tell you Maria's fairy tale now so that it doesn't ever happen again.

Be careful. In fairy tales, things are not always what they seem.

Author's note

When I wrote *Girl with a White Dog,* I was very aware that it is very difficult to stand up to bullies, especially when they are in power. That is why it is so important to stop such people getting power in the first place. I knew that if I had been in Germany in the 1930s I would have found it very difficult to be brave. There were, of course, many people who did try to stop what was happening. I have hidden some clues in the book as a way of paying tribute to some of the very brave German people who did stand up to the Nazis.

Jessie's gran has white roses in her garden. This is in honour of the White Rose movement and in particular reference to a young student called Sophie Scholl, her brother Hans and their friends. Sophie and Hans were both in the Hitler Youth as teenagers, but as they learned more about Nazism they felt they could not support it. They started printing leaflets telling people about what was really happening to the Jews, but they and their friends were caught and executed by the Nazis in 1943. Sophie was only twenty-one when she died. There is a very moving memorial to the movement embedded in the pavement in front of the university in Munich. At first it looks as if someone has thrown some paper on the ground, but when you get nearer you see it is made up of copies of the original leaflets, and photographs of the young students. Germany can be very proud of the White Rose movement, who spoke up when others remained silent.

I've also paid tribute to Dietrich Bonhoeffer, a wonderful, kind and courageous man who was a Lutheran Pastor – a priest. He had the chance to escape Nazi Germany and stay in America, but chose to return and oppose Nazism. Eventually, he reluctantly decided that Nazism was so evil that he would join a group of people who were planning to kill Hitler, but their plan was discovered and he was taken to a concentration camp and executed in 1945, the year the war ended. Those who knew him spoke about what a lovely person he was – how he was never bitter or angry towards individuals, just against Nazism, and believed that love was the most important thing in the world. I gave his name to Fraulein Bonhoeffer, the lovely jazz-playing German teacher!

I gave the former village GP the name Dr Petkov in honour of Plamen Petkov, who was posthumously awarded the Queen's Gallantry award for bravery in 2013. Mr Petkov was an electrician who had joint British-Bulgarian citizenship. He saved a five-year-old British girl from drowning, but, in doing so, died himself.

Bibliography

Here is a short bibliography of some of the many books and resources that helped me write *Girl with a White Dog*:

Education in Nazi Germany by Dr Lisa Pine (Berg, 2010).
This fascinating book explains what the children growing up in Germany were taught in their lessons and in the Hitler Youth. The chapter on lessons and text books in Nazi Germany had a very important effect on *Girl with a White Dog*.

I saw some of the text books Dr Pine wrote about when The Wiener Library in London put on an inspiring exhibition of Nazi text books and toys for children. Seeing them really helped me understand a little more what it was like for children growing up in Germany in the 1930s after Hitler came to power.

Amazing Dogs by Jan Bondeson (Amberley Publishing, 2011).
This book told me about Tiersprachshcule ASRA, a college for talking dogs supported by the Nazi Regime.

Animals in the Third Reich by Boria Sax (Decalogue Books, 2009). This is where I learnt about the decree against Jews having pets, and also more about Nazis and dogs.

Dachau ein Kunstbilderbuch by Dr Lorenz Josef Reitmeier (Dachau Art Gallery, 1995) A HUGE book I bought in Dachau Art Gallery. It is full of beautiful paintings of the landscape and people of Dachau town and countryside, with photographs and paintings of the famous Dachau Art School, which was there before the Nazis and their terrible concentration camp.

On Hitler's Mountain: Overcoming the Legacy of a Nazi Childhood by Irmgard A. Hunt (Harper Perennial, 2006). One of many biographies I have read by people who were children during the Nazi era. It is particularly good at conveying what it was like to grow up as a little German girl.

The Nazis: A Warning From History, a BBC documentary shown in 1997.

Acknowledgements

I would like to thank my wonderful agent, Anne Clark, for believing in me and my book, and for coming up with such a great title.

Thanks so much to Non Pratt and Liz Bankes at Catnip Books for their enthusiasm in taking it on and for being such thoughtful, inspired editors. I would like to thank Pip Johnson for designing a beautiful cover and Serena Rocca for illustrating it, and Robert Snuggs and all the team at Bounce Marketing for their hard work getting *Girl with a White Dog* out there.

Thank you to Dr Karim Saad, dementia specialist, for his expert commentary.

Thank you to my friend Toireasa McCann for coming with me to Munich and Dachau and being my interpreter, especially for the great conversation in the wonderful Dachau Art Gallery.

Thank you to my friend Helen Sole, member of the Great Britain Sitting Volleyball team, for her advice on the sport and the character of Kate.

I was first introduced to the study of fairytales and Bruno Bettelheim's interpretation of them back in 1993-

95, when I studied for an M.A. in Children's Literature at what is now the University of Roehampton. I would like to thank Pat Pinsent, and Kim Reynolds (who is now Professor of Children's Literature at Newcastle University) for setting up and teaching a wonderful course, and Irene Wise, whose module on illustration, (including illustrated books in the Nazi era) was so inspiring and relevant to this book.

Thanks to Mum and Dad and all my family and friends both in 'real life' and on Twitter who have supported and encouraged and prayed for me in my writing over the years - you know who you are xxxx

Thanks to my children, who have read and commented on many versions of this book and put up with teetering piles of paper, novels and history books all over the house, late dinners and endless questions about life in Year 9.

Above all, thanks to Graeme, my husband, whose love and encouragement means everything.

To find out more about *Girl With a White Dog*,
as well as discover other exciting books, visit:

www.catnippublishing.co.uk